THE
SECOND STOP
IS JUPITER

Also by

upfromsumdirt

Deifying A Total Darkness

To Emit Teal

THE
SECOND STOP
IS JUPITER

POEMS BY
upfromsumdirt

WAYNE STATE UNIVERSITY PRESS
DETROIT

ISBN 9780814350539 (paperback)
ISBN 9780814350546 (e-book)

Library of Congress Control Number: 2023933098

On cover: "Fayre Gabbro & The Queens Of Triton," illustration by upfromsumdirt.

Published with support from the Arthur L. Johnson Fund for African American Studies.

Wayne State University Press rests on Waawiyaataanong, also referred to as Detroit, the ancestral and contemporary homeland of the Three Fires Confederacy. These sovereign lands were granted by the Ojibwe, Odawa, Potawatomi, and Wyandot nations, in 1807, through the Treaty of Detroit. Wayne State University Press affirms Indigenous sovereignty and honors all tribes with a connection to Detroit. With our Native neighbors, the press works to advance educational equity and promote a better future for the earth and all people.

Wayne State University Press
Leonard N. Simons Building
4809 Woodward Avenue
Detroit, Michigan 48201-1309

Visit us online at wsupress.wayne.edu.

The Ballad of Tuvok's Barber

Starfleet or barber's
seat, it's all the same away
mission—*for me.*

In totalitarian defense of Black Innocence,
Black Magic, and Absolute Black Joy.

*For mama & daddy, for my sisters,
& for myself—my 6-year-old self.*

CONTENTS

CHAPTER 1:
I DON'T KNOW WHO NEEDS TO HEAR THIS BUT

CHAPTER 2:
THE GIRL WITH THE FRANTZ FANON TATTOO

CHAPTER 3:
THE UNDERGROUND RUBAIYAT

and the instrument lights made the beads of perspiration on his dark
skin twinkle like distant stars
—"Judgment Day," EC Comics, *Weird Fantasy* #18, 1953

She once rode a zebra to war and led an army to victory.
—Ngũgĩ Wa Thiong'o, *Wambui*

I sit on a stone
I twist a blanket around my ankles
Are you afraid of me?
It is not necessary
If you look at me closely,
you can see my whole face.
—Gayl Jones, "Wild Figs and Secret Places"

Forgive me for burning; Forgive me for disappearing
—Yoshihara Sachiko, "Candle"

I
DON'T
KNOW
WHO
NEEDS
TO
HEAR
THIS
BUT

The Hero With An African Face

for Duane Jones, John Boyega, Captain Benjamin Sisko, and Tarlton, from Earth Colonization

chapter 1 —
>   *in the basin of his helmet the black*
>   *astronaut's skull grows a garden*

as a child I slayed the dragon / dashed
through all the flames to kill the witch, ending
a curse / freeing the village / as a child I saved
every damsel, dairymaid or royal; was gifted
keepsakes by their kings, every possession kindly
offered—their coins, their crowns, their daughters
pledged their hands to me—their champion knight
& in every narrative I deeply knelt

I ousted aliens as a child / riding comets bareback
through cosmic alleys—the only astronaut who could,
until dangers were thwarted and for such theatrics
the earth thickened with ticker tape beneath my feet
making moonscapes of Main Street and at command
to my side flooded a throng of starlets gifting
keys to the city / we'd cruise Broadway in glass
carriages & ragtop Caddys from downtown
to the park, past cheering throngs & their cameras;
reporters ran through their mayors raising inquisitive
hands as I recounted each deed / the sun, soft &
slipshod above my shoulders—

"the Venusians thought weeds of us, but we resist annihilation!"

>   *—What Fine Regalia Our Inalienable Black Joy!*

but   *in real life*   I was a small tender child
a sweet black child with gerrymandered precocity;
not free to be *the exemplar* / just   *another black agitator*

2

my "soul" (whatever that was) molded into shape
by a commodifying media and its monopolizing
imagination; I was told my kind had the most of it,
this   soul,   that I should face it / that I should
take this once-in-a-lifetime adulation and nurture it
on gridirons & hardwoods sponsored by Wilson &
Adidas but   *in real life*   the Black Soul
is just a construct of White Guilt for I was born
            not a **soul**   but a **living body**

            chapter 2 —
                    my dark heart is centripetal, not centipedal

melanin, in abundance   *(or its lack)*,
weaponized into political meaning / this pollution
of some so-called   *empowerment*   as foundation
for my existence: this   **Plantation for Black Activism**
where noncompliance is grown for white academy
& its capitalism, where the theater of diversion
is sold as "the progressive stance" / whiteness with
its tactical paternalism *(the idol-worshipping of idle hands)*
branded as patriotism for all black people—an arbalest
made of empathy and their periodic table of black
mythical semen & the mystical black hymen:

            just seasoning & athleticism & crooning
            all conflated as   *Black Natural Spirit*

            chapter 3 —
                    in 2021, a launched probe circles the sun to
                            measure its breath, to touch its hem

but what we thrum isn't a drumroll for the spiritual,
                    it's only us
fed up & sad as fuck at what you've done   *(or didn't)*:
my salt-lick of language as kryptonite, the round ass
of my history defying assumptions of gravity, my lungs

at maximum capacity of sadness—   ·isn't
                    the Echelon of Soul
it's just the edification of oppression: an unasked-for
forgiveness that stifles humanity   but I never yearned
to hunger you / never hankered yielding to the taut pale
automaton of austere mythology   you see,
                    I've come to euthanize the hydra
I never had the desire to tame or pet-name it,
because   **here,**   behind every grain of gold,
                    there be monsters

chapter 4 —
                    for much of its orbit, Pluto is
                              closer to our sun than Neptune.

like every good child,
I'm only here to kill the dragons
but will they perceive any old   **soul**   *to sing that song?*

                    I—
the beautiful bard, not your soul-singing chattel,
I will not let you harden my heart as pardon
for your guilt; black skin is no physical disfigurement
nor is it the iconographic emblem for painful endurances
not like your renditions of me in my clean, black hoodie,

beneath which

          I am always

               The Hero.

          —have always been.

dark poems wobble on axis / wander into next
orbit / new worlds purge eclipse, preparing for launch,
ready to make empire of horizon—all systems aglow:

"Egun, we have liftoff!"

(but what is a "maiden voyage" to a stolen-people?) last night,
i tore off my head and from its sable pelt poured a thousand
poems—a beautifully discolored dialog with its pages singed;
my forehead ripped from its hinges, my inner voices spinning
in outer spaces like a million cosmic lampposts signaling
Elegba's ancient analog; every hair on my disconnected head
its own cathedral coiling into God's unkempt lighthouse—
the oscillation of the black bucolics, a southern philter with
a touch of botulism:

came these: this compost of neck bones as ancient beacon, a
concordance of insight mapping tongue where inner lights
softly refrain, a strobing into promise, a sloping away from
silence, the cognitive concurrency of the Soul in summit;
my severed head serving as halfway house for broken history,
becoming the globe around which my egungun safely swoon,
looking to gild moons of their own, for poems within
themselves / a home away from home where life & language
are tethered as one, where mouth and this very moment are
infinite—

conjoined.

from the black hole of a headless body
the booster rockets are falling away and
I'm sure I'm hearing roosters . . .

—can you not hear them?

I hear them   / each and every one.

Tranq Dart For Sunday Mornings With Oshun

that time we made a pool pouring
yellow paint two gallons upon the bed
our dark browns mingled naked & mired
in deep oscillating muck the coagulation
of skin against skin, a hemisphere of us & yes
eyes wolfhound red & dangerously aglow
atwitter as if hearts as lecherous & lewd
as some white-winged angel had just discovered
want & need aflutter in the dark
with Black God, jet as night, licking
his lips, inching closer:

> looking & lurking
> & inching / inching & leaning
> & nervous / nervous & leeching
> & thirsty until touch is without tremble
> becomes all-knowing. is certain.

> a given.

Blueprint For An African American Space Station

I
welcome
to my Cult
of Thutmose

      where black bodies split
           become of single breath
      ancient lovers with postmodern analog in auras
      we become brass-age with glaciers of black skin

           a bricolage of place & memory —

           please, consider this   *a heritage*

a sensual satellite I orbit you   extrasensory
                               with my forgotten sciences
        stalagmites in my voice   panther
        and mouse in the chase until   I catch you
             and become as Anubis   I fetch you

        my brown face a red giant on the horizon
        my oath to you   *a moist mothership*

as Thebes In The Night
my inclusions crash at your feet
my hubris a hybrid with debris
licking at your heels   digging
into black digital Earth cruising into impact bracing for
a beautiful burn & it's apparent—our brain cells are shattering
spooning the head of Love's Hyena-God   shifting shape
our minds blown   our mouths agape   transmogrified
telling the Thoth   the Whole Thoth   *Nothing But the Thoth*

2
I'm such the lascivious man   been so   since
                    Olodumare
seeded soul from sun and untangled man from mud   language
congeals around skin accepts gravity becomes ink   and glyphs
                              with ligatures   sinking

                    is this Alkebulan or kaleidoscope

contents scatter upon impact reprise rainbow   & leak
new gods   from un-endangered umbra   until
out
of interstellar bedrooms a budget plan is grown

            however—   *no existential dreds no backstage pass*

3
the dusk settles   carnal acts dehydrate & sparkle
                    on thighs   rate gyro assemblies
                    maintain function as we face frustum

            and Saturn returns—

a sigh-fi in the flesh   no not "lascivious"

                    luxuriant

            unbridled   unbrittled

half a million stars are probed   a million planets explored
many comets mapped   dark matter disrobes
            this   black   whole
        willfully embraced   and atop literary
                    perturbation theories
                    we build   *a space station*

        Orion's Belt replaced by Octavia's Ash

       and yet   there is still much debris
to sift through   Keplerian ellipses for us to drift into
our soft brown plait of limbs   the implosion

     of skin to this   Event Horizon

      but   *all the while—*

Our   Hands
This   Embrace
what else   did we need

Rocket No. 9 To Venus

admire me (or not):
the offspring of Sun Ra and Fantomah;
my Blues-given name: Lord Soarsirrah!

Mr. Black(Hole) Moses :

Lord of Lawds in this Jungle O' Stars
Star Train Commander and
another stark futurist in soulful fellowship

title rank: Rom Cornelius
with chevrons in my dancesteps

I oversee the archeoastronomical,
this weigh-station:

Halfway Hut for Heru's Boss Children

I float souls across deepest space like it was Styx
uplift these souls like I'm the Second Coming of Stax

through black space to a place for blacks.

this undernebula railroad of trans-libational poetry;
this libration of black language expunging a *Brookes Plan*:

I would've group velocitied more of us
if we knew we could travel faster than light.

yes, indeed, the second stop is Jupiter—

our chariot a celestial cab traveling a callow way,
a rugaba-centric leaning towards the light;
a spatial self-im-prism-ment . . .

our *dawn magic* won!

yes, yes, my dear, sweet, sweet egun; we've done it!

(*wait!*　something's amiss—***the fuel light!***)

* *rerouting* *

at the next shooting star make a legal u-turn;
there is hydrazine at the next ejecta / a full moon
　　　in diaspora;
refuel then resume travel;
carry forth for 30,000 light-years;
then carry on for a lifetime:

this *& only this*

is the quickest route to get up through.

Spaceship For Sale

2020 was a light year for you.
off-drive, every word dropped
from warp and here you are:

a world away. . . . kraal, home;
stop, alien, your urn-sitting for saturnalia.

"your hooptie starcruiser has a busted thrive-shaft
plus you're real low on anti-frieze & dark matter."

      Prometheus is an okay
      mechanic, but he's no Ma'at

it felt good when Starfleet degreed
you, but what's a PhD in astromystics
to the amoebas in your motherboards
baptized in nanobots?
      —the future is hypnagogic!

but you still have to eat / so—

SPACESHIP FOR SALE:

the tachyons are in their indigenous
casings | there's a hitch in the clutch but
no glitches | alloy rims | and there might
be a ding or two on the railgun's side
panel but no worm holes | factory parts |
never been piecemealed; As-is.

—Sirius inquiries only.

I'm what they call a
gawlologist—means
*One   Who   Weds
Pretense   To   Parable.*
Sentence structure is
my baton / twirling
iambs   &   tossing
vintage wisdoms high
into the air, caught like
a wish behind the altar
of head with a profuse
tongue; I snatch science
from the nonplussed like
a dead language, but I

don't rely on hope—I'm a supplicant surgeon & there's no mendicancy to this mysticism / I don't deal in lack-of-faith or lack-in-skill—*I'm dopeshit fareal, playa,* **believe that** / my portfolio a new age mojo bag, a kinda *jujusynthesis* and the headline on my 'nations sack says *born under a bad moon by profession*—the apothecary* of my lips: *blue in green*

contract is void if seal is broken.

my sinuous slang slays a bull / each poem pools in a puddle of blood / a coagulated colloquialism where breath is facsimile for afterbirth / there are cowries in my excrement; my physical word—all oxtails & onyx and there's infinity (*if not adinkra*) in my bottomline—poet writs a wight collar / is a blue colored collard worker / is a black hollerer / a barking hyacinth and because my butterflies are prone to bite my fabulism warrants a fine print—

CAUTION:

Blackpoet conjures on a closed course; **please**, *don't try this shit at home.*

Bleeding The Calf

-i-

"it happened here" I say pointing to nebulous inkstain
where throat was split slitting me into new language

a black rite leaving deep serration to voice's black vinyl
anti-opulent, the onyx spewed, a crude Niger Delta sludge

spilling from jugular veins and this sacrificial lamb
you see before you became a southern laureate; a vodoun

dadaist / an argot-futurist, my dark surrealism written
in slang; age-old conjurers came and bled the calf

—*what could I but comply?*
culled me, they did, from the obsidian pooled at their feet

where dust-, dusk-, and dung-covered hands drew signets
in the gelatins they stood in, commanding dark algebraic

emblems to stand & recite a science—then them / these
stick figured bones stood up, becoming me; they danced

and I became a one-man museum / a country ring-shout
walking; a nation throughout not just a nation within.

and now, my throat like a jar preserves the tar from
a borealis. where old eclipse (in all temerity) heals every

hieroglyph hidden deep like a tonsil in the mouth
of space & time, these entrails of witticism—

> *cup your hands and sup*
> *from slashes / bring Tupperware*
> *if not calabashes / keloids occur*

from where the cosmos is smudged;
the rouge of roux in my every word,
obeahs for black pidjin / a conviction
for the canonically absurd:

-ii-

where dawn is denied a body—a coruscating
genesis: its nascent tongue & vibratory marrow,
the flora of the open palm closing / the anti-entropy
of my bleating heart—this nosegay of poetry—

    I sit up in bed, the calla lilies in my locs on fire;
    I sit up in bed, an array of shadows in my lungs.

this lumbering dark is dense and aglow and from
some inner event horizon: the mirific comes prowling.

This Kiln Isn't For Everyone

1

Old Brother Hubbard did it / setting
the mood / swaying the heart until our clays
together tangle / polymers in every crevice
the mortars of romance in service of Heaven

Olodumare, our idiosync potter & master martyr
doddering in love churning omniscience into
a spackle between ribs / dear god, the sweat, the heat
of mythologies at melt / Deer-God, deliver us to Love.

2

the doggeral black womb is red dwarf / a star
collapsing into kiln / my mouth / a centaur seeking
your center of skin / an imbecile's orbit / the sweltering
genesis swirling just under breast / our love, My Love,
isn't for everyone. we are Nephilim / bareboned & Nubian
our names have always borne A Love, my love.

3

it isn't the slue of foot Fate allows stumbling
to privilege—to catch (mid arc) a shooting star
there is practice and pratfalls before sin might reek
of permanence / a pure & caustic stench / with
the staunches of fire nestled in the manifolds
the quatrefoil of love pumping fire into the mold
into this forge / of course / of us / not unlike *Sweet
Freedom's* love for revanchism—an oboism, if you will

o   [REDACTED]

they once offered asylum to the Sun then said:
Yes Your People Too Can Fly   But You Hancocked
A Waiver So There'll Be No Romanticisms Of Africa
Anywhere Alabaster Is Enshrined—so "Odeing Black"
Is Therefore A Breech; Bottomline: The Constitution
Wasn't Promised, But Duressed Or Not You Signed A Contract.

in myth, you forego indemnity in The West before they underscore
one's validity—or else, *good citizen,* you scrape for life in a vacuum.

4

humanity is the eyelid of the sun / blinking
the dawn greasing our palms and history dusting our
palms in more history / to say "the sun shall rise"
is to believe it ever sets / this crescent of sun: worshipped
by jesters while its secrets shape the court.

John Henry Says I Am Not My Hammer

(a.k.a., To Boldly Go Drylongso)

Starfleet said: Ben Sisko, take this rubber mallet
& beat back whatever hordes come haunting. but pull-
ing sigh-fi from a 'nations sack Ben replies: "Yo,

> don't sweat it; your mission statement was always in-
> sufficient as you lacked the *Enterprise* to ex-
> plore the obeahs I obey; by your design
> it's always autumn in my captain's quarters and
> I'm sour'd replicating April on a holo-
> deck. I'm not plagued with Qs or sentient quasars to
> overcome—out on the fringes y'all gave me—*what?*

> *Quark?* so, from this day on I'm a warpdriving man
> and I'll not be your surveyor nor bricklayer
> anymore; the Gamma Quadrant deserves a wide
> berth tho I seek its thrill, but with serial sad-
> ness I take leave—I mean, for Emissary's sake,
> I raised Jake in a damn hovel!—still, holla at
> a playa when you see me in the streets—peace out."

even in the dead of space, a drumming; the same
astrological summons (as to all others)
gnaws his bones & with the deed to the Defiant
on dash, Ben's forehead gleams with extant galaxy.

As The Universe Yawns Brer Rabbit Spins A Yarn
—A Kwanzaa Carol

Sundiata hung himself
with Christmas lights (it was an accident)
the tinsel hanging from his toes

his brown skin peeled away and the egungun
swept down and got him; felt him around the edges
of his human foil then opened him up:

                sardines-of-soul; his
                inner stars all spilling out.

this is the gift he gave of himself
to all the gods in waiting; Auset was the most smitten.
complete flora in the feminine. she sang for him
some Cesaria, a little bit of Mahalia, hummed
for him some Miriam, and some Abbey . . . his ghost,
this Sundiata-Star-Fish, came back and kissed Auset
       she kissed him.
they kissed each other / they loved & fucked around
& made a child

became, just they,
an enclave for cosmic rays (like all Good Egun)
became The Dark Matter for a Cosmic God

to honor the birth, they buried
a thousand cowries at the corner
of Côte Noir and Robert Johnson.

by pathology they named their child a hybrid:
Octavian Bapoto* Damascus Jones.

                *disturbance;

"behold, she, our alley-of-dry-bones baby;
our small volley of prayers & dreams!"

the adult Octavian would become a doctor
of spiritual illnesses. she married Myrlande,
an assistant pharm-tech from Haiti.
they wrote several books, plays, poems,
& essays and died together happy.
they lived forever after after living.
Sundiata couldn't help but smile out loud;
everyday his legacy was the eulogy for union:

blue jays spun down from outer space
to build nests atop the stele bearing
this story; laughter hatched face first
from every egg and funeral pyres
turned into freestyled sonnets:
the iamb of a geechee isle

together, they beat the band:

poor Black Pete on drums, Brother Miles
on horn, Brer Rabbit on thumb piano
their teeth (and our souls) covered in kohl

once, a hard rain cancelled this existential parade
but Sundiata never stopped celebrating

that's what we love most about him—from
his shed skin he gift wraps his ghost via podcast
or twitter post or carrier pigeon—Sundiata plays
the grateful host for our sorrows and our joys

Our Beautiful Black Sparrow.

he always has our back

even if we never Aché him after we say Amen . . .
but that's our cross to bear and entirely another
story to tell, the happy little heathens that we are.

The Death Of Olympia
after Édouard Manet's Olympia, *oil on canvas*

you've slaved, Sweet Queen, toiling at the feet
of empire / your heels to the fire but

Negress
—you are My Nation.

you, my love, are my lady-of-the-room,
my odalisque in apron and sackcloth;
more flora than the emperors will ever
secure for themselves. soul by soul scar
removes scar; touch us, tar-like, in embrace

in embrace the black form is ablute
a soot and silk in joyful longing
thronging absolutely in touch.

of Olympia? they won the bid to lay her
in soft display, breeding bedbugs as she
craves her allowance of figs / she cries
in her sleep and mourns like Vesuvius,
her smothered lamentations flowing
into pillow / the poor thing—this
Holy Matriarch Of All Pillows
—is not ours to concern

massage her, My Dark Sage, in rosemary
and thyme / this thistle in our eyes;
tend to the care of her abject porcelain,
basting breasts and ass in the plumes
of privilege / this rubenesque pot roast
of a woman—marinating in your hands
—awaits rotisserie.

change her bedpan then turn her on the spit

line torso & thighs with russets & celery
but do not bruise the flowers in her hair
or the apple in her mouth / braise her skin
in sandalwood & rose petal, stare at this
blemish until she blushes and mistakes
your evil-eye as jealousy or as invidious lust
—the hopeless (if not hoped-for) infatuation
she is trained to desire

curtsy, Queen Beauty—*to* her / never *for*:
      "mistress, your nightgown."

with contempt hidden beneath your brow,
bow low . . . await, in patience, her hands;
heel at the hind of this sweet fruitless pear—for
soon, primed by your penumbral grace, she will
know you both to be a Sorority-in-Servitude
she will lay your palm within hers, believing
the Sisterhood you share her own creation.

hope that she smiles but if she snarls—well . . .
we do what we must. remember, O' Queen, our cure
for rabies / many breeds have bitten our palms
but she, too, must recede (as all)
into that compost for concubines.

to that quickening, go and see the cook,
her countertop a cooling board; offer to dance,
a game of chance or chess—to call & respond:

      "the rook stands in defiance"
      "and the lowly pawn machinates"

in her cupboards, behind the blue poppy
and the Spanish saffron: the hemlock—
a satchel of laments for a basket of hibiscus;
return in sadness to your mistress, that fleshy
heirloom wasting away with pillows & plumage piled

high with goblets of wine in that room-for-whores;
smile and nod. curtsy. be polite then purge her anew
with the paregorics of midnight / this dark epigraph
pitched into her lilac'd ear as she sleeps:

> forgive me, O', Olympia,
> fair Lady-of-the-Lake-in-Training,
> but I have no life to lien you.
> poor little Tramp L'oeil, spoiling away
> waiting to please until pleased;
> I clean the moat and you float on feathers
> but I would not ever trade knees with you.
> despised, yes / indignant, yes, but
> I'll not be lowed by your likes / made sour
> by your looks; farewell, fair thing, fair well.

alone my love, you rule the roost
and very few will think you, moon cricket,
to be so devious . . . dismiss her with care
then race to me / and I will halo you
—because scar removes scar.

behind our walls of thatch and moss and tin,
we two usurp a throne—courtesans of the dust . . .
mouth-to-mouth we are magna carta / magenta
& soot / jesters bray in dyed laughter & gawdy
robes, but every peacock has a claw to cleave
and to cut, to have and to hold:

> that is why I lionize you.

all of my poems pamper us;
more than love, I do not come to you
to merely "adore"—with yearning idolatry
I burn their god-forsaken bibelots
in the braziers at your feet, broken and raw

for Priestess, you see:

I'm   your perfect pedicel;
          prefect and pagan.

and if ever I come to you a useless vessel
then reduce me in the figs, the saffron,
& that hemlock . . .   roux me

until in every song you pearl within.

A Blues For Eunice Waymon

Eunice Waymon couldabeen
my woman the one with
the wet breath & warm shoulder
"baby, lean here"—a lacquered breast
"baby, cling here"—a verdurous lap . . .
Eunice Waymon couldabeen
my better half but i got hooked
on facetious praise and pie-eyed
prose *(plus, yes, i was way too young, but still)*
a man couldabeen half Osiris and
half the son of Shaft smoking Camels
and riding a giraffe, taking her
to the backcountry for us to
cul-de-sac or chicken coop
      • our caravan of many shadows
      • our pillow talk of acceptance
& cigarette ash *(and i don't even smoke!)*
yes lord,   *I wouldabeen*
her true love—you see, **my hair**
was the right color and everything.

The Second Stop Is Jupiter

- 0 -

there's no place like home, but
you're not in Kush anymore
are you, *Dorothy?*

when making love, leave room for levitation.
bite down, but not so hard to break the skin.
when using other utensils: consider the tongue,
the torso, the collarbones, & shoulder blades.
in emergencies, the nape, too, can be a handkerchief;
every makeshift limb a floatation device.

   lol:

     GIBRAN &
     LORCA &
     RILKE &
     NERUDA &
     UPFROMSUMDIRT
            —the romance classicists:

     their extant kisses
     a complete collage

  Liar, Liar, Rants On Fire!

- I -

as a child, say of 24 or 25,
your body is still a bellows. there is still
the tint of video game to your voice. your "love"
is a hoarse whisper; coarse, incomplete, and
not yet losing hope. your every poem as rambunctious
as some heavy-headed goat with curved horns broken
28

and butting brows with common decency
           (or anything else that moves)
you've not yet grown hooves although your beliefs
all chew tin and in your sleep you become
some other people's misappropriation / they ask:
what, after all, does a doorag even know
about fancypants let alone *a happily ever after?*
tho, conversely, what even could the west know
about Elegba In Love? for there are two participants
to every car wreck: the witnesses & the ones within.

                 - 2 -

the romance you're trying to reach is disconnected
the dialtone drones on. the palpitations are missing,
just a mono-tonal pulse. they aimed us all towards
their wonderful *Niagara* but that water just keeps
falling down & goddammit our love funnels up!
it's *Nigeria*, after all, that calls to us.

western love is all wicked witches, picket fences
and bikini clad Swedes with sweaty breasts
and several bottles of beer on the wall, but Dorothy,
when the wizard drops his pants pay attention
to the swag—is it Egyptian cotton? a polymer blend?
only in cinema do wizards wear pajamas and bathrobes
probing munchkins for protection spells; some ghosts
stepped out the bush wearing Leon Talley; oh, *Dorothy*
(whoever you are) what a mineshaft that mind
of yours, under where exists a wonderful you.

           (own it)

                 - 3 -

let love jump a baobab branch and

your bride will jump the groom but if the cow
jumps over the moon then you're in a cursory rhyme
and not reality. what you want is at the precipice
between gardenias blue and begonias black, a love
that looks like you—or at least looks like
what *you think* love looks like when closing
your eyes blowing kisses to clouds of heather
within your heart—the cardial; the crepuscular.

the cosmos is one small cavern; a crevice
that leaks god and reeks magic; look closer—
porcelain is the purgatory of most men / break it.
burlap is beneath the tongue, taste it.
its beauty belongs to you: the residue
of treasured memory; a chimurenga buried
beneath an often borrowed freedom.

like any Roman holiday this poem is
a pagan ritual praying to a love stripping itself bare,
it lays naked within itself and asymmetrically shoulders
a sun you thought existed much closer; this poem
shudders when it snows and shows sympathy
for stolen legacy, knowing the symphony
of its own skin—

who will you call *mama* once you've been reborn
but know not the poems of your mama's people?

         ‑ 4 ‑

almost an ancient, say 54 or 55—you're probably safe, your
whole heart sound; it's okay for you to name yourself anew,
something instinctive for your old innateness to know you by;
something anti-inflammatory to the castigating lips
of your aunties and uncles—or—you could just say *fuck 'em**
         and be the open sky:

eyes open;
dreams wide open.

* remember tho—the zhuzhed-up
sobriquet bequeathed to self under this
systemic haze of foreign encampment is
still considered—most times—*a constraint.*

- o (a retcon) -

Dorothy? Jochebed?   Zawadi?

Zawadi?!

Zawadi, yes.

yes, Zawadi, there is   *No Place Like Home*
but this wind sheared space is Kush enough
for us. *for all of us.*   at least—*for now.*

The Maternal Otherhood Of Mythematists Will Now Come To Order

note to self or whoever else is listening:
you dont need me to reflect you—i deflect myself;
i'm no bleached agent with secret agendas in my gourds
and you don't need me to protect you / you just
need me to knead you / & i want this to be mutual:

1.

we gather / casually black / like bureaucrats or
small-town laureates / each of us full of extrasensory
paternalism, elite externalists chasing boyhood dreams
chasing the pursuit of influence and leadership
our pimp-strut in lockstep like a learned
behavior; the patriotic socialism of an urban gulag
but my attempt is to keep my hum penumbral
and it is learning to listen / my silhouettes have
obdurate angles / my silence is softly adumbrant
but in truth, i never know how to hard sell
the sideshow that's inside me

2.

The Davises:
Helen kept her motherwit razor-sharp; not   *sassy.*
                         just   *sarcastic.*
Rother was a soothsayer with sandpaper hands
and sawdust that fell like dandruff from his shadow.
                         also   *sarcastic.*
sourpusses to outsiders, but just
two tragic martyrs on coffee break awaiting sainthood.

so from their example i'm an old southern solarium
a houngan of the not-so-humble arts so i tend to
gimcrack in freeverse giving parables in answer to every
mathematic equation: "how many underpaid pragmatists
does it take to make a poet?" / in a room full of black

metallurgists i beat the brow of Anansi . . . not anvils.

mechanics? you want to talk about mechanics??
not a memo, not a meme, not a bestiary . . .

—*mechanics?!?!*

i won't.

tho i digitize by trade, it's the cow-tail switch,
not your sheepskin, that holds me in account

3.
in a land (*oh lord, i sound like a movie trailer*)
in a land where grown black men (in order to
prosper) must be ore / i am a moot militant,
a winter's mote / the summer's spore.
i john-the-conqueroo in complete quiet.
so if you are in need of spiritual warmth or
well wishes—in those i'm adept—then
i'll watch your back and empower you,
                    that's a promise!

to be proficient in the languages
of "black bureaucrat" i learn to barter
in currencies of bravado and spotlight,
be in brotherhood with mass perception

there isn't, as of yet, proper hugging in the huddle
of America's beautiful black men / so come, bold knights,
and let us frolick in the ponds like all heroes of yore with
songs in our throats while hand-in-hand—and yes, we
still carry pocket knives, for whittle or for worse, but
not for (without reason) any random old bloodletting

        —you'll find no *cinematic savages* here / glorifying
        the curvaceous whorl of conference tables.

4.

but here i am, soulspeaking over bourbon; the arms
of our ancestors referenced deeply in every sentence,
the extroverted offering / the exchange in theories
of introspection and black love . . . every conversation
meant as embrace.

when in the boardroom, my powerpoint of gourds
present this: a renewal for camaraderie. for the sharing
of chimurenga (in real life or social media)—the pledge
by each of us to be as steles in the struggle.

to be the heroes our mamas never had until
jump back turn around pick a bale of cotton
is no longer the expected themesong
for black children come bedtime.

to walk an island of seashells within the rings of Saturn
          —protecting joy / praying to ancestors.

5.

          —*The Sacred Oath of the Mythematist*—

the haters send their hares at me
here, i suppose, to take me to Havana
or (i shudder) the Hellenic, carrying me
towards triage on their tiny cots:
me, a black fat blot on their quilts of kale
          (—*my astral sheen & i, one wonders*)
but i oppose & dream of Ancient Harlem
and if you must, you can reroute me
through Hazard (if not Harlan)
—i am rust and i am woah and i woe
but in the roe of me i thunder; tho also

          i coo

          oh, *shit,* how i coo.

Ogechi Hula-Hoops The Rings Of Saturn

Katherine Johnson, job title *super computer*,
made her cadet helmet outta graph paper
and a thought bubble; hubba-Hubble . . .

all systems Igbo; we launch in T-minus five.

now calculate this: the directrix of a Sande mask
in unpersoned flight or the parabolic curve
of the constellational vévé
on poor Gordon's back . . .

> *you can't.*

not enough prime numbers;
and not enough time travel . . .

but Creola could. her clothes hamper full
of Euclidian geometry and On The Moving Sphere
her tramp stamp . . .

Ogechi in her spacesuit with the fishbowl:
the glass helmet that condensates a fog; Ogechi
(with the tip of her tongue) scripts a love,
a poem to Blind Willie's orbital plane
and signs her screen name,

$$axe^2 + bc \, (Y \mathcal{H}) = \emptyset^{shun}$$

—page 360°, *The Ditch Digger's Guide To The Galaxy*

To Stand Down (And To Stand By)

ancestry is all I have / the only mythology
that remains / how else to explain this oscillating
darkness / my id without effort & very little
edit // here is how i show you voice—some
shards some silt / the evisceration of slang
on altars made unkind {if not un-kin} // what
else were you expecting / it was you {after all}
that hauled Kilimanjaro into Kentucky / our
pristine snows melting into an Ohio River
your fathers polluted {and now Olodumare
has his dander up} so I cradle in both palms
mounds of dirt to ears and sing along with
the convulsive slag / if I mumbled *O' Guinevere*
in my sleep then blame cultural famine, disease
or fatigue, for in my sleep I often curse // you
said "show us the concrete of you" but all I have
is soft & fertile and a need to be festive / so please,
I beg, stop gifting me asphalt as filter effect
my perspective remains away from kilter and
is seldom out of focus // then {in reticent critique
& by cultish default} you say of us / of me:
the cis black poet is best showing us his dick and you
betray me // I write "repeal" / you say "repetitive"
and neither of us can break tradition // so I bequeath
to earth my dying gasp / breathing through this
apparatus of black skin // this inheritance willed
to me // a wealth for which your purses
were never designed to have {nor to hold}.

The Night Of The Purple Moon
(Media Trial Upon The Death of Olympia)

—The Ancestors' Opening Argument:

vandals whitewashed it all: our wardrobes, our walls,
our wishful thinking / our thought bubbles made
to clean tubs & scrub toilets / made us pedagogical
lapdogs to Olympus, kneeling and praying to Bacchus
swallowed whole by Zeus's entire narcissistic brood,
telling us how a decadence declined was a better fit
than the sackcloth of Black freedom—no room,
one supposes, in philanthropy for the fairy tale.
and who cares if the chains around your ankle
are of solid gold or if the dagger they dig into
your clavicle was once used for slaying Caesar
     —we know better.
deflowerers came / foreign until domestic
contagions with their satellite dish a disposable
shrine forcing kraal-builders to raise a cul-de-sac

"go back home! go back to Africa!"

but right nextdoor our keys slot perfectly every latch.

—The Prosecutors' "Time-Honored" Rebuttal:

don't be *the ungrateful slave*; aren't you satisfied?
our pearl-handled teeth entrusted to your palms of soot;
why does sweat not suffice brushing our tresses—your
ruination of lyric, dreaming the fan of self-fulfillment
instead of fawning over our iridescent flesh—the opals,
marbles, & opiates fueling our Poets as they author God.
you sad, lacustrine echo; the nemesis unto yourself.
you hypocrite / you heathen! why, just yesterday
we fed you offal on fine china! now you dare

deny intimacy with our excreta . . . disgruntled
spirit you cut to the very hellenic core of our
ambivalent evangelism! your every rebellious act
a tenuous disgrace, your non-deference
is totally despicable and *oh, how you pain us!*
but it was not *our* hands Divinely gifting privilege
to porcelain / you lacklustering ne'er-do-well,
forgetting your obligations to the strata.
but you are not The Sun, just its victim,
equally within the frame as without.

—Laure's Closing Statement:

"before prosperity, enshrine the proverbial"

my Gods (in every variation of Brown) are in
every gourd; the sweat of stars glistens on their
night-time skin, but their favorite color's called
"underground"—they love to laugh yet fierce is
their wrath piercing your insides with parable or
a very pointy stick, whichever appropriates in Man
a self-awareness. now, i know not how to make
a hood wink or a bam boozle, but i've seen it done
when i googled "how to exit a ruin"—you simply
run through the door.

so for my next witness we call upon the switchblade
& the running shoe—their testimony of *shots:*

> at the table,
> for the title, and the ones
> around the world.

The Three Sulas

"rise up ooze, you protoplasmic Black Jelly!
wiggle your arms, free up your toes,
bend over, backwards over black words
and let torso touch and blend with sky!"
     —and with those words, i woke from the dead;
         black neon wrapped in sky blue linen

three women tended my wounds, a triphthong
of country witches—the universe in diasporic
wailing, making roost in a central Kentucky cave.

     "we saved you,"

sang the eldest, her long thin fingers
covered in pig fat and cow's blood . . . her hands
a ball of quills, gnarled & elegant, her hum
a dark caw—soft and soothing like the cooing
of smoke—*if shadows formed a cloud & cawed.*

the sweat down my back
     —a condensation of crows,
and tongue had the taste of dirt, sage,
     cinnamon—my first thought: to spit
but the youngest clamped a palm
to my face and said "swallow all saliva
or you'll decalcify and be more zombie
than automaton, ruining our recipe
for reanimation—and you don't want
your viscera untethered, voicing
(without foundation) for mercy, do ya, hon?"
—her every tooth an opal, so exceptional;
"now tell us, even if it feels wrong,
of the life you last recall."

"well . . .

my name is M.C. Lessons . . . i was
in the woods hunting squirrels for supper; i turnt,
ready to return home, and whistled for my hounds
but emerging from the woods   a white woman.
her brothers mistook my dog command as cat-call.

they bristled and i could see the gristle dancin'
in their throats. they shot me from an impressive distance
(lucky as fuck) then i was lynched . . . and shot again."

          the rope burns an unhealable blemish.

          "i died.   i think i decomposed.
my spirit melted into the soils and i spread out
                    becoming a meadow.
i was full of rabbits and moles, i was full of worms
and . . .   wormholes?   *cosmic.*
then the unfamiliar moved atop me. i became
a subdivision? a . . . *a cul-de-sac?* a pink man
in a striped suit stuck a yard sign in my forehead
—it read *vote for obama / yes we can.*   was that heaven?
i could feel the gates of hell responding."

the middle witch rubbed my limbs in shea,
"it was just a dream. a probable portent; *it happens.*
the mind breaks down much quicker than
the body and moves ahead into the earth
as fast as lightning, but you ain't been dead
but a few hours. we found you with
your face missing and took pity; broke
our oath on you against raising the dead."

the eldest witch was weeping reachin' out for me,
the cow's blood sieving from her sleeves as we hugged.

"what happens to me now?"

"shit, you wash up & go home."

"that's it?"
"if that's all you want, yes.
tho youngest Sula here is still single."

     they chortled
     & coughed as she winked

"now, your squirrels are in the river
but you'll hate meat from here on—*sorry.*
you'll thirst some days for yams and raw
unseasoned dandelions and wild animals
will talk to you, braying poems, in your sleep
—a small setback, but you get used to it;
you'll be fine.   besides, most beasts
ain't too talkative, *'cept them damn geese,*
they never know when to end a tale.
anyway, your horses are out back but
we'll be keepin' your dogs as payment."

the clean shirt they gave was the same
worn by the first man to shoot me.
"don't question it."
her pipe in hand, the eldest witch's grunt
was guttural. she smoked pokeweed & begonias.

"scurry 'way, you small soothsayer,
you orgasmic spittle of sun; wiggle free
your arms and free your toes; ascend
every rainbow as you quest; be capillaries
for the supernal so when you learn to call
for dawn Legba will know to answer."

—twas two centuries ago;
i've been a poet ever since.

The Astral Black Baedeker

1.
meanwhile   10 years later
the moon grows larger / fat   with dystopia

why do our bedtime stories have ashen sheens?   the sex
          &   the soot of it   beneath eclipse

Amos Tutuola's ghost   offers its hand to   us —
     a slow plodding rabble of abstract black absurdists
          trapped   in this paranormal paradise

each of us a time capsule   isolated   our ghosts
                                 guiding us   from misfortune

          to freedom   to facsimile

2.
the growth-folks home is at capacity / capsizing
to a youth too bored to brood / their civilization silver-coated
a faux place like homme / a spritz / a son of a glitz spray-painted
over bloat / over indoctrined commonality—the intersectionalities
of oligarchy, nationalism, & Armageddon

          welcome to bedrock:

          forgive us if the 21st century oversaturates;
          it's not a misnomer / it's just a mistake

the sun shunts to the side then we slide towards
a baptizing bedlam / an mtindo wa sanaa   or *jugendstil*
so worry not for this end of the world if you want
but every known apocalypse (as of yet)   has a sequel

                              / ghost stories

with   the   puppy-face   filter

3.
───────────────── ~~lesson~~ lessen 1:
                        your ad here

4.
                        lessen 2:
                           DM me for more likes

5.
wait.   this wobble is too consistent
        perhaps we've gotten off on the wrong foot
        all these weevils and not enough cotton
        to the weight   of our enlightenment

so here / to break the ice i wrote a joke:

a vampire, a mummy, and a werewolf walk into a bar . . .
the vamp shows off a Brazilian wax and says
        "you know what? I'm a writer!"

        "no shit!?!" says the mummy

                ba da dum   / joke over   / get it?

the werewolf always waits his turn   yearning
for inclusion / cue cards embalmed to his palm, he says:
        "in real life i haberdash without punchline;
        my tv show is in development."

6.
sign scrawled in the bathroom stall:
                        i'm just here for the Wi-Fi and
                        the refurbished   disco

7.
our hero hands to us a dead sound

haunched over and scratching   at hunches
                no punches pulled   culling
            cleft   from   clot
his brain stem rotted   while mulling
over   every   letter   of   the   truth
                but who cares about the truth?
                you?   yeah, right.

in commercial capitalism it can't even be used as currency.

8.
canonically   or ironically   we've all
~~become the Wayans Brothers   as white women~~
                gone the way of the Ancient Mayans—
            the white pearls of modern lit coming to the aid
            of black maids some 60 odd years ago in six-figured
            publishing deals gifted to the ninnies they once nannied

every sigh is self-professed   / hubrises over-exaggerated.
a conflagration of swag   in fact, if you want them
                                 to take you serious, then
every sentence is a social network animated   / if
        you want them to not mistake you for
            the unreal reality has become

9.
to be fair, the newsprint this poem was written on no
        longer exists
                                 / *POOF!*   says
the literary magician   spoofing   himself
but   fact or fiction
who among us   maintains faith
                        in a gutted Gutenberg?

what a canon-drum   *this amen noodle*
                fund fact:
                        newsprint oozes now
                        a binary brogue

44

10.

pop quiz:

   all who think   *conflaguration*
was misused in "stanza" eight   please lean   to the right
      if you agree with its use then to the   left

please leave the room if unsure or unconcerned which answer
even matters / keep that contamination to yourself, thanks . . .

besides   anyway,

            i wasn't going to pass you

without a bribe / blame it on the "climb-it" change   / on
                    Felicity Huffman
ruining your grand entrance ~~exam~~—and even with
all evidence in   accountability still escapes
the Gatekeepers of Eminence; Society still scapegoats

                An Ethnic™

while Naked Ambition frames the game and holds contempt

                        for the gameless

11.

                  lessen 3:

the successful samurai is a sultan of penmanship / such
is the kernel of calligraphy—to be chief caliph of letters,
the longhanded, long-winded poet . . .
       today / we just txt #anshit   fr
dissertations for a Lyft driver's PhD / imho

chosing the raunchy over Rashomon and that's a damn shame
or a god dame . . . *or is it a damn sham?*
i guess it's *magna est veritas, et praevalebit,*
           no metaphor too mega.

12.

wait,   *it wasn't a werewolf!*
        it was a dinosaur!   . . . oh, shit!

i ruin the joke until funnybone has no legs to stand
and yet you always seem to laugh

                              you always laugh . . .
but *at and or with—*   any laughter is out of place

                can not the black poet wax woad
                until somber & surreal? until
                silly & nonsensically unsound?

        a Frankie Evelyn & Waugh or Tome Wolfe?
        to Gorge, Oh Well, like a Hunger S. Thompson

                see—*IT'S THAT LOOK THERE!*
        i did not come here seeking knighthood from your sobriety . . .

this is why i never really liked you / you fail to give good eye
and that, that makes you horrid as a reader.   plus, you have
spinach in your teeth   and *(can i get this off my crest?)*
i find it disconcerting—you, sitting there—*drudging a book*
by its author.

Elmo shrug   *flower emoji*

but it's because—*suckee to sucker*—us sullen literary
antagonists (shameful as it is to say) still want your love
is why *i had*   to write this / *"my intro to let you know"*
a voyeurism / a heirloom of history beyond
blacksick vaudeville & blackskinned revolutionary

        a hagiography / a preamble / a field guide

        —*a grimoire*   on us bumps in the night

        plummeting headlong through adventurous dark.

46

Meanwhile, Near The Moons Of Pluto
S3, Ep2: "Our Hero Runs The Gamut"

I.
the entire planet is a black man's backpack,
an entire bookbag this foreboding world.

tho as a child it was my Sputnik:

back to the grass, face to the sun, the complete
planet my sail, my engine this great starship of
a planet with me—captain & pilot and every
crumb of the cosmos on my shoulders.

to neighbors i must have appeared playing possum—
flat on my back / legs in the air 90 degrees bent / feet
adjusting pedals they couldn't see; hands attacking
levers / driving invisible steering wheels
for this terrestrial projectile called *Home*.

2.
"Sphinx of Black Quartz, Judge My Vow!

these aliens, hideous by nature,
they . . . *theeeyyyy* . . . they shall not
defeat me / i shall *never* surrender . . .
never shall i be the pet prize
for their pale, alien desires! i will
leave them wrought and adrift
in the wreckage of their own
'*unconquerable*' claims,
abandoned in their own hermetical plight;
their myths and sciences a diminishing
flotsam in the wake of resistance.
wherever i roam i am free / immune
evermore to the decrees they think divine!

forever shall i defy them—*forever*

i shall *fight!*
fight!
fight!*"

3.
an innocence, even now, that escapes their gaze;
their souls consumed with unshakeable blindness;
the fugue / this thundering aphasia / between us.

*THE
GIRL
WITH
THE
FRANTZ
FANON
TATTOO*

The Annunciation Of Fayre Gabbro

the seafoam in the teapot boils over
—a tea party for Black Barbie Mermaid

Chukwu opens a steamer trunk with a skeleton key
—the sky roils out, the backbeat of the basaltic

a sleeping car porter explains the concept of horizon to a sea-slug
—mindblown, it assoils itself, singing *together, are we not oscine?*

violets & cowries / legumes & thistledown spill from dawn
—the celestial is but tinfoil for the mortal miracle

& from The Old Bag of the Night: Erzulie ascends
—she is vertex of Heaven / spear & shield / a zebra beneath her

pellucid and black and loyal she always was
—a buoyancy of all the things light as air / as heavy as hope:

the passerine from the abyssal
—*wee caesura in crucible of moon / sliver of monolog in maternal crescent*

Chukwu, Sweet Phantom, says Erzulie, *I am deep with Child.*
—a mzimu, a lodestar, emerging from a quantum dot.

Fayre Gabbro & The Long Time Coming

the abacus wept in its wait for Gabbro:

Grand Nne Akuko Ifo *(within her Gilded Bubble)*
sings floating above her court of hens & chicks, riding out
disruption / her magics moored to the Gossamer Moment's
upcoming tale where—*centuries later*—Nne's lucent halo
a supernal bauble turns cat's-eye & rolls down an ave down
the urban gutters with fauna of Black Folk in toothsome lore
—each glossy soul a mossy ode within Esu's legerdemain

  —Fayre Gabbro, Agbogho Mmuo, Lady
  of the Golden Interim, *before ascent,* consults the cosmic:

  Q: "how does the Sun outlast The End of Days?"
  A: "whether dawn or dusk, She just keeps breathing."

until nigh is now and begins at last *(like any affable fable)*
with a nine-year-old & her Big Wheel popping gum and swaying
from a path of angry jays until she topples *(in prophecy)*
to the ground where the Gewgaw of Gabbro / objet d' orrery
or vito kupatikana with its shimmering skin rolls into the child's
amber palm / like a propitious grain into the hands of Fate
where its ore cracks open as if an egg *& out steps Gabbro:*

    her crown of flame
    her gown inexorable with daylight

raises her wand & clears her throat—*bestowing*—and as foretold
(tho once forestalled by primitive force) we all begin:

the privilege   of *Once Upon A Time*

        insurgently glowing up.

Fayre Gabbro, The Girl With The Heather In Her Hair

Once into a space

Between the maidenhair & the blackmagic hollyhock / amid the dew & the dawn a wild was born / a stark bioluminescent child / a small barb of raven's wing birthed in heather / a slushing slurry / a dislimning folk song / a fight song / nebulous & delicate / the macrocosm in infinite cooing / a tiny wisp / a gasp / a bituminous fawn—*Gabbro rolled out the bowers* / from the very apron of nyctophilia into the brawny arms of this *new-entire-world-in-waiting* / a tuft of coal she was / huffing & puffing / full of solstice & sulphur & solid gold / *once upon a time unto them* / into a space a wild was born / a herald of the aequinoctium / half foundling / half celestial / a bright 'n' dainty harbinger of the full life we all desire under this inscrutable Heaven / this spatial baldachin held over from our Egun before—*before:*

once upon a time

Fayre Gabbro In The Land Of Isle Iffy

after Carroll's Alice, after Tutuola's Ghosts

shrink into sun / the blue sky slung in your kitenge gown
feet-to-ass towards moon / full stop at beach / out a whalebone
door beneath the sand / its driftwood knob—open portal if
cursed & shadowhaunted / if distraught & seeking shelter
stepping down into Soft Heaven's black oceanic palms
a calm wine tinkering within the gourds / a balm—*blam!*—for
the mad chatter from the dread blight of the sad haint's white hair
escape the night as a queen of hart making domino
of constellations weaving through nonplussed wonderland / your
saga of hexes / your caterwaul a pillar of ghosts

Fayre Gabbro & The Spindle Of Somnolence

to lay in sleep, the hidden heroine-to-be, with
a wreath of daisies above your nebulous coils—

(the queen's kisses where you pricked the lance
& spindled a curse) a nosegay of nightshade

bundled in soft palms folded over ebon breast,
the green earth at your nape, red clay

for a sleeping tongue, the pleated light
(through every bough) falling gently across

your brow where all of God's God-Given Brown
belongs to you; 50 yards of kente & lace like

a nightgown of forgotten language covers the
fields (a small fragile genesis); your bone marrow—

appleseeds after obsequy; O' Gabbro, how long
will they heedlessly drowse you? with field mice

& faeries nestled in your hem / a duvet of northern
wind above the tome of you while a million wards

away your quilted horde awaits—a lilting girandole,
an omnium-gatherum of Mass Mysteries Unwilting:

this Orchard Of Stolen Tenebrescence, ready
for a Princess to awaken herself with kisses—

her dream of self & agency until it happens:
tender Tutu, Argus-eyed, in Gabbro's Castle In Spain:

"Get up, Gabbro, abandon this gilded breakfront;
they may no longer bind you, placeheld in menagerie!"

—after denouement, a blackness is dawning;
the sun in your eye until by end of day the story

unfolds, our renascence for a slate that no longer
slumbers, (as foretold) dismounting towards

Ancestral Prefigurement with blue jay & corvus in
confidential muster like a cluster of omens pending

ascension or regency, your resurging luminance
above all—post-awakening—with bloodlines risen

and Hypnos (& his sand-shilling henchmen) alarmed
in his bed— the morning cock *(the informant of gods)*

as sudden adversary, ceaselessly crowing. and
this is how Prophesy asserts itself—with the keen

blade of sword shielding your gaze from Fairytale's
harsh warning / surging with eyes incensed inside

the softened shadow of you beneath your crown, facing
the days ahead the dead—*dead wrong*—believe stolen.

The Weening Of Fayre Gabbro By Amma The Holder

-one-

my hands are not large enough
to keep you; your shawl of skin
across the shoulders of night

the ovum of sun in your smile;
yes, my hands can not contain you.

the volcanic, offers to claim you,
to call you its kin but there is
no concept of horizon at the hub of space

and then some say to leaven you—*you*,
the inseam of all solar systems—within
a single Earth, but it is undeserving
of your catalysis and if not even within
my hands then how possibly within
some ashy trinket of dew & dough?

you, Gabbro, are too good of a goad;
so i'll hide within you an Eden:
a boundlessness immeasurable

your tree of life within my vase of palms
so i shan't embrace the tenuous—preserving
the cogitative baobab within
the institutional bell jar, a phantasm
akin to shaping vascular dimensions
within the ledgers of performative prose . . .

never in stasis / always in a stage of genesis:
my hope—to hide you in plain sight
to make you soft, delicate, and durable

but not for the debilitating dream
of grand romanticism's narcisstic lens—
i'll make you the Nebulous Patina on the teeth
of Abstrack Futurists—placing
no limitations on allure for the interstellar;
your Classical Beauty
                    —*a timelessness.*

-two-

my hands, at times, unsustaining;
both palms porous so by consequence
            this cup runneth over
            is by intelligent design

so here you are: the peel &
the pit of the big bang / forever expanding,
faster than life, larger than living and
as combustive / as utopian as any thesis
from the throat of the empyreal finch
                    —*a despotism.*

The Fever Dreams Of Fayre Gabbro

the sun stares down into the mouth
of the poet and she says *you never ask me to moan*

that's because a kiss completes us
heat rises from the earth, melts the snow
& wets the leaves.

nothin' up my sleeves says
the ghost lothario; running hands
through tight meandering hair
& barks out—*africadabra, baby*

    Forgiveness pops out the body.

dandelions dream themselves
on fire for her / the look of love.
the lamp of lap and the dawn down in
the frozen lake waiting for the ice to break

two bodies braid into twin shades of brown
if Orunmila will share you i will bare to you my soul

there is ligature and there is literature and
when we are bound we are both

cherubs in the ashes / satyrs conjoined
in the science they share / this reliance
on the myth of how they master the unbreakable;
their unforsakenable bond like a pond between
two rivers; two givers fond of love

a body bears down / stark eyes staring down
darker eyes staring up / the phantasm
flaring up—organs on the rise & on the run.

voodoo hardwires the software;
adulations & spells & the penumbrant,
a punditry of the luminous:

> we are spittle
> of sun / wherever
> we land we sizzle

smear me, she says, sunbeams
for forearms, a deep sea in the lower
body—a nighttime privilege.

mindblow'd & bodybloom'd / all
consumed in softness / fingertips a plethora
of pagans; hellhounds & the devil howls

and   baby,
         you smell good to me.

adrift on a breeze / a black dove over
rivers & flower winsome dark

hallelujah! shouts the heathen
(the hoodooist), his clean hands within
her prism / her wreath of Wound / an
heirloom of poke weeds & wrought iron

their entire shadow reaches 'round
the earth, becomes as marrow for sunrise,
the plein air of blackness.

every star looks down into the mouth
of the poet, i don't need you to sing me, she says
we only need to grow ripe & awaken.

Fayre Gabbro sits up, sweat-soaked
as the moon through curtain gauze lowers
himself into the room / its warm growl

drenched in honey—

> *what a tender courtesan, the cosmic,*
> *come to billow beneath my gown;*
> *but if you believe in Us, Dear Darkness,*
> *then return & enter me in the noon.*

Fayre Gabbro, The Woman In The Sun

1

i was twice a Coke bottle in a catcall
but mama once called me an obelisk
and i liked that / a column of stardust
or wanderlust as solarflare / a radiating
sapience from when Self straddles
the world dark & holy / the flame
in my shadow with its memory of feathers
my cadence of breath (in or out) a black
bird as from a poem
like a proper gawlo i am drawn
to innerlights / where i stand my
slender frame forms a squishy tower
of sun but i've always been the muse
for the light-flying night moths nicknamed
Queen Mother Mothra when love
is in the straightaway / notice now
how the dawn as if sedge surrenders
at my feet—*Young Highness Acraga Coa:*
puddles of silk in my lambent lungs
watch this gracile gargoyle crumble
from the thawing of her curse / broken caw
dispersing into iambic song / nothing
squandered — if i am coarse it's from
a hoarseness in my perspicacity avoiding
the goetic and its Cimmerian entrapments

2

i was once a caryatid in vociferous pratfall
bullied into acquiescence within
the odalisque's amphitheater but
you can not harness dreams carving sunlight
into harems employed then beneath horizon
like tombstones for art & literature's
decaying gods standing in all eternity

as mortar to your exclusive gaze
                    yes:
my back is a straight edge but i am no
simple ledge of granite / however whoever
first describes me in reckless affection as
a tender tuft of moss or a fawning stalk of ochre
then that such cotton-eyed purveyor / curator
of the butter-sweet myth they have the chance
to win me over—softly / voraciously

3
as the dreams of surveillance lay dimming
i rise—self-symphonic / black mondo in
unclaimed beauty but wherefore art thou
Liege Ego "Independent & Strong"—otherwise
a Denial of Privilege & Community by any other name
so come hither sweet maiden grass—i as well
surge with regency and deserve many
counterpanes on which to swell & swoon

4
not just a Coke bottle
          —coquettish
          —the coqui

Fayre Gabbro & The Sepia Pudge

"Mme DuVernay, I'm ready for my close-up."

the sun burgeons—a long division
between terra & the divine
this flourishing solar afro marking
the birth of genesis / a praisesong
of Yahweh from way back—*drylongso*

Love is a bouquet of apertures,
so—O' *Dramatic Romance w/ Sepia Pudge*—
lean into this lens, your depth of field
unfurls & curls around the soft dark diameters
of my nape my lips and upon the tiger-stripes
on blackthigh in my theme song

       my dark garnet among foliage bright
           —a vignette that fights against the grain

I'm photoshot among the ferns,
my carbons embraced by frame of Day,
my shadows feathered in your exposures
until, like *Yemoja from Her Clamshell,* I emerge

so come, Sweet Ray of Light, and linger
on every pore / within the wild tarragon
of my hair, your observatory turned a hothouse
your telescopes trained tightly
upon my portraiture's Bear Paw Jade

—in the forehead / this phylactery of Black Literature
          the morning comes uncollapsing—

the morning fidgets & slips from the phalanges
of nighttide and where intimate vistas develop
my latent image appears—an elegance, blandishing

& uncropped and where I'm the most dusk the sun,
beneath this softened chiffon, (within my silhouette) surrenders
a blackness so dense as to be see-through & celestial

and like any happy ending
I'm iconic to every camera as tranquil pussy-ear
might appear to you in your unremitting palm.

The 12 Labors Of Fayre Gabbro

she slits a wrist to let the lions out,
    naught in seeping but tentacles weeping.

the sparrows stuck in gutter's downspout have
    drowned, their cadaverous shrill her theme song.

the voices in her hair in labored hum,
    their murmurs in soft lament of beauties

no physical accord evokes without
    aversion's enthusiastic consent.

oh, luscious sorrow; oh, opulent death:
    alabastrine words clabber in the throat.

Gabbro's disentangling spell, her graphene
    vow clears Ogun from such soft, grecian urns.

The Colluvial Interlude

it's not fleeing / if it's freeing

it's not fleeing / if it's freeing

it's not fleeing / if it's freeing

> if it's freeing,
> stop running.

if it's freeing then it's not fleeing;
it's not fleeing if you're allowed to be.

> and it's not really being if you
> know not how you belong.

Fayre Gabbro & The Colluvial Eclipse

they said you were too dark
to be a damsel in the tresses
too hue to be diaphanous—
our smythes could never coax lore
from such coils / anvils in distress!   said they—
        the foreign fabulists
but   *I love you.*
I've always loved you / my Sanctum Obsidia
soft & fragile / floral & igneous / my *deep blue calla*
            only / **come**
escape with me Fayre Love fresh
into Heaven's Colluvial Eclipse / this
verdant embrace like Twin Stars of Thence
                    / I love you
Miracle with the Mammatus Coif / 4C & 7
million tears ago   */ **I love you***

                    / I love you.

mischievous & whimsical / too dark
        they said
to be pert perky & dainty / perjurers—*all* and
with my castigating tongue I indict them each
& every one with my vituperating fairy tales / only
escape with me, Gabbro—Fresh Maiden *Dark & Dewy*
—bell hooks & Belle Brezing / into this *Umbral Universe*
where kizmet and adventurous peril awaits

            the *Us & Us* of it

with every inflorescent keloid in full meridian
with all this laughter & soft nourishing love
a sweet sorrel fleeing deeply into our pores

Fayre Gabbro & The Preponderance Of Love

"the deepest grade of blue within my vowels, affixed
to a de-memorializing limbo / a dimming purple. a deeper
whim without hymn or perfect homily with your name
a lacquer on my tongue: an anomalous beauty. your name:

      a bouquet. a beehive. a blackest resin;
      the heavens coated in sublime ebonic calibration;
      your amalgam of locs a luminous tephra.

<send text>

this bright random error eclipse. <send text>
this bellowing / this beaconing. <send text>

our tongues conjoined / twin comets streaking
extantly through sky; our kisses—axils of the reimagined

      our compounding silhouettes a syntax

<send text>

oh, the transversity!   can this be love?

and here now i hover denying & daring—just *DARING!*
our mortal existence to fecklessly dissolve; an exact cataclysm
that neither of us can abide."

<sending>   < . . . > < . . . > < . . . >

Fayre Gabbro & The Flowers Out Back

for Kutu & Shanita

I've stayed in the front yard all my life.
I want to peek at the back
Where it's rough and untended and hungry weed grows.
A girl gets sick of a rose.
—Gwendolyn Brooks

she watched her mother feed on weeds, the roses out back
growing rough, just as the sentinels intended, but Gabbro
grew tired of such sickness, this cultural illness passed down
through generations like a family crest, as sword & shield—
the societal balm for the provocation of her natural beauty.
"beware being The Princess© in public," an uncle joked in
warning, "best to be their prized mule and they will love the
labor of you, but, woo-chile, never be the virgin bride riding
bareback or the-unicorn-they-can-see; the poetry of those
poachers will call your teat milk 'gamey,' your Hottentot ass
mounted in the Freemason's Hall where all within is lumber-
jack's plaid & hunter green with armchairs of grotesque leather
and yet not a crinkle of your hair to be found in the boudoir
of the chalet with the furbelow and the arabesque bagatelles."

and thus, in a thunder clap, it was decided, to be
neither yah-mule or The reproductive mare, but
The Lady Gabbro: *The Blithesome, The Beauteous,*
Our Maiden Most Sincere; the decolonizing third-act
occupying the restorative nature of privilege; explorer
of provisions hidden deep beyond the pale.

wherever the countenance of color is unbearable,
a forbidden bane, then Gabbro will be a centralist,
the darkest aethers of phantasia reclaimed / destroying
The Classicists and their dominion of **Onceness,**
upon which Time is a vassal / this oppression of rubrics . . .

"I Am Here For All Of This," she will say; Queen Corvid—
Gabbro, The Rectifier. The Futurist. *The Fairest Of Them All.*

Fayre Gabbro & The Cumulus Conqueroo

Fayre Gabbro sits in public transit spittin' rhymes
in Ebonics & Gabonese; Water Melanin.

the #7 Downtown dissipates / the wormhole
is bright & warm; this is the subway to Saturn.
all fares paid, both ways, by Cassius Clay's
Olympic medal—the eternal ATM
at the Ohio River's murky bottom.

Fayre Gabbro disembarks on the outermost ring,
met by The Houngan With The Penumbral Fro,
secret agent for The Society of Cumulus Conqueroos,
to utter his name without proper reference to the cosmic
defames him,

but they form a congress, these two, a two-headed
council of wizards & africadabraists, a two-manned
crew of C.C. Riders, LLC.

"my lady," he says, lifting her to his ride, a dromedary
with two sets of wings and a single curved horn; they
do not hem & haw / he & her, they   adore each other.
                              they   adorn each other.

and thus, embraced for adventure, they ride
destined for The Nebula of the Wayward Negress,
where 60558 Echeclus was last seen:

The Mystery of The Missing Comet!

two CRINE Scene Investigators in umbrant flight / lovers
& smiters / devout evolutionists (the both) . . . to their core.

The Night Hawks Fayre Gabbro

after Edward Hopper's Nighthawks

seeking console i haunt solace in greasy spoons beneath sick neon
oil churns in hoary caffeine each cup empty of lucid nirvana
formica frames me holding frigid dusk at bay eldritch but idle
in unsolicited privilege my genesis for the serene
drowns lament in lukewarm coffee before arcadian geniture;
softness has epiphanies haint is ample with heft atmosphere form
within now barking soul stillness births a rattle for matriarchy
a luxuriant luna-ness enriched by the presence of eclipse
tho a dark globule i'm irrepressibly bright within soft umbras—
a lamppost made holy by shadow's uncontainable night brigade.

Fayre Gabbro & The Black Fracas

long ago & far away—

it broils / her society (under the skin) / as
murky as it is mercurial. asymmetrically seething;
satan teething on her spleen / degeneration
giving birth to the Secret-Agents-for-the-Unseen©
deeply seeded within her viscera . . .

with such a roughshod anger,
Fayre Gabbro is Heaven's Aorta.

tired of sipping tea, she shatters / her percolated
spirit exploding against porcelain's bright attempts
at restraint . . . she's the lull in the china shop
tired of being nulled . . . she rises off the ground
—every Orisa inside / *Rocket No. 9 to Venus*—
Fayre Gabbro rises from the Earth / ~~a hurricane~~
~~in a teacup~~ the dystopia in a gélé / a daughter
of the dust made hypergolic, a Patternmaster in
the making . . . Fayre Gabbro is a pitch tar patch
in a sundress, is Butler's Brooding Lilith:
the tar leaking from her teat, she says:

>   *all I ever wanted was to know love and to share it*
>   *with all who surround me; to roll around in this*
>   *Odd Creation, frolicking in the maiden's hair and*
>   *the dahlias and the dogwood's fallen blossoms . . .*
>   *the buxom beauty in tenebrous delight reciting Rumi*
>   *& Reed / Madhubuti & Keats into the podcast app on*
>   *my smartphone, but no; y'all motherfuckers here / y'all*
>   *motherfuckers / everywhere. this phallic fallacy. this*
>   *progressive gaul with hipster's beard and the waxed*
>   *mustache of grande-ole-pay-tree-archie. oh, my kingdom*
>   *for a time machine to go and build a wall around*
>   *Vespucci, making Amerigo grate his fucking teeth.*

Fayre Gabbro swoons, the back of her hand
against forehead, she sways and falls into
the chaise, sackcloth on its surface, but like her,
stuffed with moonlight and stardust and
mermaid's breath; she repeats:

> I am dainty and so ethereal it pops my melanin,
> a darkness so soothing it makes me diaphanous &
> **ain't I, too, a Romanticist?**—so fair & velveteen
> I'm Goddess Obsidian, black & urbane as ever;
> even my machete is highborn and genteel. this
> realm so enamored with Queen Alabaster that any
> soliloquy in Iconic Sloe is beheld batshitcrazy, as if
> dignity is not indigenous to slate; a fit of anger
> does **not** demolish refinement it only diminishes
> one's organized monopoly to such definition.
> in the corners of my hearth—an herb garden;
> releasing fractals of God in these tendrils of smoke—
>
> my bones be branches,
> their marrows veined
> with gold; and if i cannot
> soothe on your shoulders
> my daunting tears, if not
> your handkerchief to
> soften my gaudy weeping,
> then i'll seed this earth
> with sobbing songs
> & wring my face
> of lightning
> until reaping.

Fayre Gabbro In The Orchard
after Privilege and Romanticism

in adjacent droughts they laze a Wyeth field
like heifers with attentive palms out for borrowed cud
spread-eagle or prim / demure / afloat in ponds
among the fronds / dainty jowls nestled
in knightly palms—those wild windrow-of-a-woman
over there with windswept skirts basking the lawns
in allegories of sun / intimately begging for recognition
if not salvation but we here carry our own wheat as raised
and there is so much ocean water in our walk that everywhere
on earth we settle leaves a softened flora once we're gone
—lithe gardens in a sable grove working twice as hard
for half the adulation bearing from our forbidden limbs
the most resplendent fruit / the Gods of Ancient Orders
dangle Romanticisms in our pliant branches and Heaven
blooms in these slender boughs—even in our undergrowth.

A Lullaby For Fayre Gabbro

she's like a djembe that way—with its belly hollow . . .
        paunch struck

but where else for it to hide the palms' dissipating echo?
        not hide. but to hold.

her timbres / taut & haunting.
        dense & dulcet but always lilting.

Fayre Gabbro Meets Her Maker

O, Great Rhapsode;
O, Divine Mshairi

knuckle joints acrackle with *Incipiency*,
take me in thine hands / cradled in the inks
of Juok nestled in the creases of the speckled
argot of poetry—center to your cackling palm,
my song the anther to your stalk of language;

elevate me in status *the tongue-in-between*;
the black & blue roan your nouns ride upon
with the forlorn fable of Schrödinger's fate
for inside your calyx of verse—

i am *shorn & unshorn*

for not all prophesies are known
by the people; nor even all parables;
not even known is every poem
—*the hero*, it's said, *sometimes* **fails:**

her primordial song left to stew
in some laptop's digitized dusk or
dustjacketed in the cobwebs of broadband
for a seldom-used desktop;

her workaday shadow decaying / her
prosaic beauty revisited in slant rhyme
as exorcism for the *purpose* of poetry
(*and for its pretenses of)*—an apotheosis
that paints by the numbers / but still,

O, Grand Inquisitor,
you self-absorbed cad

berth me in ode your beau ideal—

the dragon in the caul / a foal of summer
in the hymnals of spring / graceful

in girth & lank / a keloid of many
bevels / mysterious / your discordant
manifesto / just hear me out:

   if only in your head:
           heard & here'd
you see, within your hoard of pages
i am my most hallow—so bring me searing
not to black lit as token for the auction
block / witless for restrained pallor's
judicious system of rewards / for i am
deeply profound within your overweening
poems / even if, *in ambitious prosody,*
you choose *(or not)* to eat the farraginous pussy
of the themes (beyond measure) you dream
about / it's okay, baby, to be coy, if not
the coward, your commonplace kindling
too damp or raw *(in your mind)* for
The Institution's commercial foundry

—tho just how many gateways can a poet's
pearly teeth, in verse, stand in proxy of,
preserving lucid canon's grand conventions
like a robber baron?

well, sir (whether bard or minstrel),
i will not question your motives
or motifs should you strand me
here uninquisitive—my black body
brooding an eternal dawn / bloating
purple with the yolk of morning

   —a horizon hidden.

however,
when not altogether forgotten—my life
does pulse across the canvas on your
slender whim so don't leave it here
     lightproof   / a lie
in decaying mercy to your temperament,
a purgatory in battery-powered limbo
voltless within the aethers of this
cloud-in-virtual-akimbo / yowling in fancy
without the force of material voice

    Dear Tenebrous Maestro,
paint me in a corner as you wish
but i beseech—don't be cruel

     O, Poet . . .

tho there is phosphor in this bronze

    i dew / *i really dew*

but only once observed & before
that by—*your entire spirit*—embraced.

Fayre Gabbro & The Duppy Of Dreams Epistolary

you're not from around here

> *yes, I'm within a dream*

i'm within a dream as well
see—the clouds are calling
the stars refuse sitting still

> *perhaps we're within a poem*

then we both are as fawns?

> *yes, we both are fawns, such is true*

this love then a temple?

> *our love, yes, a temple*

and we are light?

> *and we are darkness with a hydrant*
> *of stars, a living coal within the clouds;*
> *come hither Sweet Kite of Harrowed Hope*
> *and carry us throughout the sky*

how proclastic you are in beauty
revealing to us the future

> *a perpetual lux; our sorrows peeling*

the wick of tongue

> *our alphabets trimmed by sallow wax,*
> *we break the dim of flaxen language*

a signpost ahead, severed limbs forming arrows

> *"This Way To The Soapstone Castle"*
> *this dream is both chimerical quest*
> *and fay cogitation!*

no this was always a poem
when were we ever not the syllables
for an overlapping song?

> *this long-lost syntax of embrace*
> *romancing a renaissance*

to be lost in Langston if not Elhillo
if not Farrokhzad or Osman

> *so Gwendylonian to the touch*
> *a Finney for your thoughts*
> *to be Fagunwa-like, black and-*

Ngugian as ever, graceful & comely
like Alice In The Bush Of Ghosts
paying tithe to a vassal of bones

> *down the houngan hole*
> *with our mad tenacious chatter*
> *a Cheshire Himes*

Check the Rhime of the Ancyent Mari Evans
drunk in the privileges forbidden
the spiritual osmosis of privilege
with our oaths munificent to gossamer & melanin

> *yes we too can privatize a lyric*

a prize or a peeve

> *no capricious lore of others to travel at us*

no facetious fable

> *a lore that travels with us*
> *perhaps even through*
> *proof we are not trapped by dreams*
> *and the industrialization of hope*

joy lingers beneath the rib
unfolds into provincial laughter the pollen of light

> *we must indeed be floral!*
> *who said we lacked nectar to our veins*
> *with fairy tales barren and falderal*

but which came first, the quickening—

> *or the powder keg?*

we are as one a bouquet of poems
each pore a village of children
vessels of blood branching through the nimbus within

> *this is how we raze with voice*
> *apotheosis in the breasts of Onyame*

and yet they keep asking Occam of us!

> *how parsimonious!*

their philosophies on skin a speculative slogan
with embroidered stats a congressional claptrap—

> *reciting history with dehydrated jargon*

but there is no desiccation to praise Gabbro
drought has no wings for the likes of us
we skim the core of a nascent earth
unsnared by the nets of Ogbunabali

Anikulapo: our slang is incessant
gitchi gitchi ya ya

dada—expositions free of enucleation

you are a poet

we are architects
we scaffold the sun

        to drift asleep in Her Great Adumbral Bosom,
        to awaken as dawn over soft republic in the
        stadiums of commonwealth, tiers upon tiers

you are from here

        we never left
        not a once

you closed your eyes and found the dark

        i found an echo
        or some annunciation
        a duende deep within
        and when i open my eyes
        to augur the morn
        i catch my breath
        and we double down.

Fayre Gabbro In The Fenestra

after Lucille Clifton's "if I stand in my window"

I'm as nude as a quasar
on the floor of my gundam
spread-eagle in the peonies
my thoughts a spiraling galaxy
of poppies & chrysanthemums
even my railgun is marble & pearl

I am twice the opulent—the naked
aubergine of my body black in nacre
within my gundam clam every jalousie
& blast shield opened wide & wild hair
hanging down like an ancient fiddlehead

margarite drips from my burning hymn
my cosmic song of joy & longing—
a thematic romance running far-flung
throughout the streets of space & time
and every opposing canopy abandoned
within the resonance of my shadow.

Fayre Gabbro & The Trickster God Dossier

- i -

the goblin king, injured and hiding
within the bush with hellhounds hot in abundance
turns to his small companion, the child Gabbro,
for whom is his charge and helps cover his escapes,
taught her he did in all the ways of *The Whimsical World*

the tears in his eyes a roux of his soul / the goblin king:

injured and angered with iron teeth in his giant
head, talons of great graphite, his tongue a cocoon
of leathery gauze with spells fraying on his lips

his milk-quartz skin as white as a unicorn's hind
and his wide bulbous eyes the perfect verdigris . . .

"*Fayre Gabbro, sweet lass, it has come to this,*" he hisses, "*haven't all my poems come bifurcated, full of ooze & fur? did i not teach you how to handle the poisoned spindle? did i not tuft your ears from the dove's murderous coo when it came blaring with rotten hymns in its bill? even now, the raven-queen's quill juts your septum in protective augur and just the other day didn't i teach you to read the globe of the hyena's skull when lost in a woods devoid of moss? did i not compress for you the entire floating kingdom of Blasse Träume into the bunny tail puffed neatly beneath your crown? and the cadences we sang in joy with dolphin and crow after rescuing the serrated ode from the terrible toad with sabered teeth & melodious breath; our adventures in Conch City, Little Lagos, the lost caves of Neptune, the Black Hole in the Tunnel of Light . . . what a full life for barely a teen! but i am a goblin, The Goblin King, and i hunger, and to be healed (as is known) a goblin must eat the heart of Man; I'm sorry, Darling Waif, but i must consume your essence, your nectar—its melanin. it's much to ask, i know—the abeyance of free will, the sacrificing of self for the perpetual well-being of your betters! i won't bore nor bother you with details (as gory as they are) or how pained i am having pledged to protect you from ever seeing* me suffer: much is my love for the memory of us. so don't cry for me, but recite softly—for the soothing winds—the first lullaby i taught you lifetimes ago, then close your eyes & i'll make it quick, without trauma—The Swift Ascent!"

the sharp crackle of his flinting teeth;
his dagger a slow-moving sorrow, a long lumbering
ghost song rasping from its sheath . . .

Gabbro, the queen-child, with the knowing smile
her hand calmly in his unfurling claw like the pearl
safely in the clam; his paw scratching for skin, finds
an ossifying ore; an unscripted moment of laughter.

> "Sweet Friend, i was never the fool . . .
>   as a child i was given many doors
> and dreamt this day a decade ago
> and have walked each morn since
> seeking forgiveness that softens.

>   to buy time, it's my Spell Of Rambling
>   that hinders your healing; chanting
>   transmogrifying rhymes under breath . . .
>   even now, your feet are mostly flora; your hand
>   more prickly succulent than a fist of saws . . .
>   your head more cabbage than crown . . . I'm sorry,
>   sweet liege, but when the devil-dogs arrive,
>   they will find only your aura in atoms
>   & spores; your dissipating spoors drifting
>   over the fields. the *retired* Goblin King,
>   Shepherd of Ghosts and All Gardenias."

"SANS SOUCI!!!—you pawned me!
you ingenious, igneous pearl! you alchemy without peer or flaw; you young blossoming enchantress, you pussycat—the vegan soucriant with impeccable rapture. after 800 years i am finally pinched! congratulations, dear all-wise champion-of-me, to you i tip my crown. your thaumaturgy is complete for i am out cast and must now view Creation from The Balcony Of The Sun, my secret ultimately revealed: Unoka; Unoka is my spirit name; wrap it, please,

in hematite and in suffusion add it to your coffers between—the carnelian &
lazuli. in full clement (without rue or worry) this King of Heathens is dead,
the prophecy true; may the spirits grant his proper heir a grand dominion and
a crescive acreage in the capitols of Heaven: Fayre Gabbro, henceforth, at ei-
ther dusk or dawn, my shadow-slang's at your behest & haints alone for you,
for you, Fae Trickstress, are the new Guardian Of All Gourds!"

in many facets a faucet of tears befell
his golden vest, by now (on the surface)
a satchel of seeds, as the princess places,
in respect, her snap bean wand against his
chest—a burlap in decay & growing green. . . .

- ii -

Fayre Gabbro weeps
a river; Unoka's name
& all his pollens—the tessera
for her gris-gris
to this day still.

John The Conqueroo Asks Fayre Gabbro For Her Hand

be nourished by my word.
be cherished; never narrow us.
i will never ouch you; watch me.

a perspicacious sight: dainty,
atramentous and true. and this
aegis'd fable is my sable oath:

i am anikulapo for us, i swear. and
once professed, it means the dawn
will never dim while i have you. and

i swear
to fuckin' god,
i have you; i will always have you.

Fayre Gabbro Invents A Truth Theorem

Fayre Gabbro in the infinity pool spits over
the edge, her Chanel clutch full of soapstone,
devil's claw, slivers of iron, reams of daylight,
some mummia, the expensive bag bobbing
at her side and is not waterproof; the tattooed
wadjet on her nape winking at the stars; the Eye
itself describing what's seen inside her to the egun:

> this mermaid has feathers and a fur
> coat. her black wings stretching out
> like an underscore on either side. *open,*
> she says, *and take this diction, there
> is no eviction, not here, to our beauty.*
> awe-mongers made obtusions of her
> softer sloe; but now that she embraces
> it / they object; in blind allegiance she
> builds, in our image, a shrine in honor
> of all shadows:
>
> allusions of Gods-In-Love for all to see
> and for that they call us "Heathen."

Fayre Gabbro & The Three Sulas On Her 16th Birthday

(the countering of a virago's curse forced upon Gabbro at birth)

SUla // for thee, a **Scrying Skin**, all who stare will be
mirrored within; they will self-reflect trapped *(like motes
in amber)* to the nigrum of your gaze and they will sigh
& weep & cry. they will laud & worship, then they will
abhor themselves—this longing—and they will cry

SuLa // for you, the moon will sway; every sea,
Fair One, will kneel—the **Aquatic Hull of Your Heart**
a summons, a broadcasting beauty; your love a soft
and tender conch with its deifying touch, the tidal
dawn of your arpeggiastic African touch

SulA // magma in the black body is misread, *yet still,*
yours will be the **Crucible They Cry For**; you will forge
for them a swailing; the molten swale of your affection;
your searing, emulsive kiss—the immolation of all restraint
to your inheritance *(where neurodiversity is a sacred isthmus)*

aside: *Gabbro kneels & makes in secret her fervid wish—where not even in published
stanza is audience owed access to dreams; so, one by one, each candle is blown /
every slice of cake / any song / all joys quietly divvied; but we won't here mandate
privy to a young woman's sagacity just because you read poems about her or feigned
a fawning, slipping 50 bones into a vestal maiden's Cash App on TikTok; no one owes
you the blueprints to their underpinnings—not even in this foray of dark verse where
the black poem is allegory for the liquidating mythos of contemporary lit / so, please,
I beg of you, My So Enchanteds, don't* (in the entire waking world) *ever choose
to be that creep.*

—fr fr

The Chiaroscura Of Fayre Gabbro

for Jackie, Deborah, & Karen

> *—toward*

the halcyon comes with reckless hunger you
ardent shadow / your hearthstone arrayed in half
sensual song you delicate umbral purr you coquettish
congolian falling star the noon rises into you knee-deep
in fauna at wander in childhood fable / a fervid
moon with widening crescent embracing awn

> *—torrid*

swept within the vestiges of romance you kitten
you teardrop in damp seismic skin lush & unabandoned
you parable you paragon you / you / the veiled comes
and nestles full hearted in your kilns like a wet supernal
breath an auric condensation where black nape is
most distilled a yessing desire you dark throbbing
bijou you flickering cinema you saturday-soft matinee
sun-drenched until desire falls moon-blind

> *—torrent*

undrying with broaching cameo slushing undecantered
& muted beneath frail inquisitive dark the coming sun
a canvas of want the morning gouache collapsing
into the night-crusted furnaces of you / queen caesura
of all rhythmic thumps in fallow night you bright
impeachment of dawn this confluent love a burr owing
itself to every oil haunched beneath your awnings.

The Fayre Gabbro Palimpsest

4.9 | 6.7 | 5.8 | 4.8 | 5.7

i was undainty at the cotillion
azure & adrift in unsanitizing shimmy
was born in sequins but said
unspectacular by several judges

they measured the distance of my eyes
from the bridge of my face / measured the width
of each nostril, stifling their laugh, then labeled me
Queen Mother Mare and laughed outright
when fitting me for my gown. they said i was "cute

for a giraffe."

4.7 | 5.5 | 6.0 | 5.3 | 6.3

seven layers of Burt's Bees on my lips & elbows
and the curve of my ass / princess of the proletariat
—*has anyone seen my potato gun?*

i am soft & harsh
& not too hard with my heart.
eat my zest / i peel in your palm.

7.8 | 8.8 | 9.3 | 9.5 | 9.2

& stop looking
for reasons to not love me

9.7 | 10 | 10 | 9.2 | 9.8

the amber waves of grain / the cheese grits
the charcuterie board / the broken headlight
on your time capsule / and as Pluto is not a planet
mac 'n' cheese is only a side dish,
motherfucker / you smallish, manish man . . .

the overhearers equate our laughter
with happiness / born into my own hands
the poems i write are already centuries old
but i was never a gymnast
not without my words

"dear sweet, heart: your soffits are weakening."

my tongue is a catwalk for fire
the tongue is its own selfie
there is no fire escape from the tower i've become.
this "window to the soul" is no exit
the way out is in vain
the handles all turn to little or no use
i looked for love & you gave me a latch

8.8 | 8.7 | 8.8 | 9.2 | 9.5

i am too delicate to be your fist
writing was always my roulette
my head aflame is no frothy harbinger
feared / it's my fragile mercies
tenderly ignited / I'm a brunette harvest
from head to toe

i venture towards the misbegotten
the disenchanted depths
the unrequited heights

the blackest love language
as life support / the fishbowled
breathing apparatus
the tissue of sun unspooled
& unspun & stuck
to the bottom of my spaceboot

:: i am fearlessly soft ::

o' the worlds i have lain to waste

you there with your sneering eyes
& leering hands come hurling fast
and unhold me. . . .

8.8 | 9.5 | 10 | 10 | 9.8

i did not travel time simply to jeer
at you i came to rescue
the Master Weavers
my whole body
a loom of love / the nunchuks
unsheathed / the jackknife already
in midair / Steve Rogers, the squire,
tosses my shield to me / this spear
—mama's favorite keepsake—
i cradle iron like a family heirloom

before liftoff i stuck the landing
so come & kiss me on the lips
this dark, diaphanous thing
this translucent ore that swallows
all light / the chiffon fraying
at the edges of my gossamer
kitchen / this obelisk i call
a neck / this thick nappy

troposphere on my shoulders
you never lacked the words
your imagination is inactive
so i weep at you for your ragged
Christian upbringing filling the gap

it's well known you never intended
the uneven bars be so level
my skittles a steroid in your gaze
your gaze a sprung floor as i dance

but we control this lutte
this laamb is mine

9.8 | 10 | 9.—
stop. *please, stop.*

it's who romanticizes our bruisings that breaks us.

The Coronation Of Fayre Gabbro

concrete is not your natural
sheath. say it. so many petals
were boiled to death to make
this stew of you. in this single
spot the sun shed its skin & broke
itself in half to spread you with
its marrow. say it. the lunar
gulf of your language washing
away their ordinary magic

i am cosmic awake
and i am cosmic asleep.

this slithering spell
of a black body, cool and coy
to the touch. moist in memory.
so ancient hymnal for a new myth.
goddammit—SAY IT.
all this faerie dust where fire
touches skin. lean into the sternum
of my story—*SAY IT!*

this torchsong,
this fever blister,
this pussing black boil
glistening with love that praises you
and achieves a dominion of self.

this west african echo;
this black epistemology.

sleek and smooth and as soft
as daylight. this permafrost
thawing on the heathenly tongue
this shadow steeping in its own

sweet, cane . . . this tree bark, this
meteor-pocked, dark roast
coffee bean of a woman,
this goodnight titan with
the mudcloth doorag,
the constellational stretch marks
and the civilizing teat.

a breast milk of palm wine
& sorghum; i said   say it.
open your teeth and bray it.
your throat a busted O-ring
gushing like nigerian oil these
songs of ascension dancing
straight through a plastic eclipse
angered by the natural corona
of your naked, blacked-out cameo.

Fayre Gabbro & The Wond'rous Expanse

Lady Gabbro, in darkness fair with
wreath of hair an Untamable God
lounges with feet hiked atop her bed
back to the floor / staring straight through
the ceiling to Havens Beyond Heaven; her breasts
flaring against gravity like a Clifton Blackbird,
arms in soft repose behind her nest of hair,
fingers, egg-like, scratching into scalp, hatching
a supernal sound / the maestro of midnight-songs;
the cross-stitch of Ancestors, their bellows
in her belly. her heart a comet without tether,
her love a blue whale leaping a celestial sea
with spiritual pulps lapping the shores
a deep blue leviathan skipping o'er space like
a pebble flat & smooth, her soul a blue dwarf
with the ablation of space and time; *a Romanticism*
without sorrow or rue, Fayre Gabbro is replete
in beauty, A Complete Splendor Dark & Undormant
Queen Cobalt with sepias warm within drifting
into a most Wond'rous Expanse—and this is where
we meet: acacia growing wildly in her teeth
her blushing gaze a crushing quilt, her lilted
laugh an autumn breeze, a captivating blush
of coffee on her blouse heaving as we speak,
her entire being an ancient altar / Hoary & Rapt.

Fayre Gabbro & The Fuckboy Who Too Late Sees The Light

we all seek ablution he says
our palms wet with adulation
soft damp kisses between each knuckle
a momentary tongue blessing the life-line
the veins at our wrist throbbing
with insurrection our devout followers
down on all fours stunned and weeping

this is my want for you in desire of me
supplicating and destitute my body beveled
at your knee lips brushing your brunet heel
until broken in two by ample beauty my sentences
agape and draped across your ankles my body
wide open for your titular decree

how catatonic the heavens above
now seem crowning me as i drown
within you and the fauna of your supple behests
my mouth full of treatise the adjurations
of which you forbid me
even now
to swallow

Fayre Gabbro—the lenticular ghost
waters mountains aiding how they flower
her bare hands sluicing sky until bare sun
pools in each palm ponds for a bigger tomorrow
sup or bathe or not crave or not
but Gabbro will not be drawn & quartered
her radiance carved into someone else's silhouette—
the property of cops or robbers or rubber barons
of grown-ass men old enough to know better
with their vulcanizing eyes their misophonic love

Fayre Gabbro & The Dragon-Faun
(A Scene From The Kente Book Of Fairy Tales)

with leathered wings dragging tempest
the imp-austere plucks her like a black
corsage from the castle's turret—his bone-saw
of palm, his weathered clutch a claw-song;
the young iyalode *(per her wish)* surrenders
in joyful swoon, happy to have him; his talons
reduced to tinsel, his fangs tangled in follicles,
dissolving until lank within her coils as his *(or
is it hers?)* bifurcated tail stirs an offering of tea,
the tassels on her whiskey flask trailing
in the wind like a panegyric above the city;
the machete, given by fairy-godmothers,
resting gently under boubou like
a counter-balance between them—

   the wyvern purrs *Gabbro, i thought i'd lost you.*
   she thrums, *Deer-God, you never could.*
   —and that is how their caption reads.

the horizon above and the horizon below—
the both *(from a distance)* appear so dark,
a storm? perhaps; her laugh—a gossamer,
an oleander that lingers in the light; his aurora
under wings; the silhouette they share a foreboding
fog while far below: *the gilded prince*
with his holy entourage point & stare & beat
their swords, cursing the night; their failed
fabled gentry as sorrowed dowry, demanding
fealty for a love never theirs to command.

The Canticle Of Fayre Gabbro

This rock, it hums; this clay; my tiny
Heart as flipbook within a walnut shell
—a compositional sparrow in timid flight

& from my straggled sleep the coming day is crooning;
Antiphons ringing out like sunlight spilling
From the pores on my palms—**Gabbro The Canticle**

—My insights profoundly cyclopean:

My hands to my face, these hands running down
My shoulders—communiques between skin & bone
This self caress as user agreement, an update between
Marrow & breath; a bleeding epiphany where joy touches
Sorrow; the trees *(outside)* nourish darkness in their limbs:
Seedbed for the figmentary, a hothouse of shadows
For the Gods yet to come—a nucleus *(to some degree)*
Of the spiritual candescence from which I seek comfort—

A dorsal sun launching from my spine;
The divine trembling in my roe

—& wades
Uncontested
At my behest

Forgive—*if sounding cryptic*—as self-incipiency often is; so,
To clarify (perhaps) *in the one true slurry of language you know,*
Your sallow guile informing hubris to ideate this:

A caryatid, self-aware,
Returns from death
& walks away.

Nanan Bouclou Requests Of Fayre Gabbro An Audience

float down, dear feather, straight from Nyame's
mouth with all your ancient geology;
how old, by the way, your stack o' stones?   *how*
odd?   you old continent in wander; with
bonework of interstellar cerulean:
a medium full of hydrangea,
carbon, hydrogen; you constellate in
purposed transit, you night-flying comet,
a *consistency*—burning scar throughout
the stratus, a psalm that heavenly streaks;
voice of zodiacal cloud, a softly
deciduous song exposing to us
your inner-working climate with nothing
left to us in chance by the void in the
cold. land here, you bold, doe-eyed downy thing,
from the sainted hands of Gwendolyn and
Lucille, withdrawing from the motherboard
your capacitors of cobalt and gold;
how many ohms, by the way, your voltage?
you vintage verdigris, you astral dust
storm of caraway, and sugar cane, and
perhaps a pinch or two of turmeric,
you Flowering Viola—celestial
berbere buried down within your form
like the sinews of a star; this throbbing
umvelinqangi churning within the
coils and the quills that hold us, hand in palm;
float down, dear sweet ephemera, land here,
& here, &—   and if for no other want:
then for my wish of a shared appetite

                    you soulful xylem,
                    siren of desire.

Fayre Gabbro & The Reclamation Of Time

a sonnic

> *Oh, what'cha gonna do? Without your ass?*
> —Sun Ra, "Nuclear War"

for mortals and fairies alike, the blood
is a powerful machine, the dirt of
it coats the celestial flooring like
the nebulous dust bunnies under the beds
of gods, is the darkest matter drifting
between planets and moons; blood ash, naked
to the eye, is the language of suns. Fayre
Gabbro holds her prisoner by the scruff,
he, kneeling down in tan, torn Dockers, his
head over cliff, the sea crashing below,
stark waves seeking dominance, dominion
over the living world like a vast, wet
shadow seeking new skin to claim. to slake
it, the only way, is with sacrifice. . . .
Gabbro, sundressed in yellow, machete
in hand and the sky a surgical blue
a mourning hue humming far above her.

> *who am i to hold disgust in my core,*
> *clogging entrails with centuries of shed*
> *skin not even mine, the world's debauch'ry*
> *ruminating like a cud or cancer*
> *within my soul. but i will not indulge*
> *intemperances (beyond my doing!)*
> *taunting me as my own personalized*
> *theme song / my organs infested with the*
> *cloying voice of my captors; reception*
> *of such solicits unkindness within.*
> *i once asked we coalesce an amends,*
> *but you sucked your teeth at me in default*

and this is the recourse you gave. having
lapped us for years before allowed the run,
our ankles clabbered by law as you laughed
citing in anger / calling our lapse in
pace a clotting drag to democracy;
your profit-mongering / your greediness
dressed as paternalism for our lack
in progress; your abhorrent wealth absolved
of historical context, your gold coins
wet from survivor's alabaster guilt

   but the crocodile
   tears that sate a thirst is still,
   yes, a malfeasance.

i was not born here before you to be
the guillotine; dear opponent this is
a politic, you placed yourself here, down
at my knee when you came in the night for
my kin, my elders, our flowering youth.
heartless but not thoughtless; a choice. and in
my own anger i respect it, but there
can be no waver to an already
wobbled world. this isn't revenge, think it
a correction in the curve, the pit buffed
from the surface of a glazed cylinder.
and the crow sitting rapt atop your heart
shall heft you anon to a brass council,
toward judgmental accord damning you.
but i don't hate you; i love me. the end.
the bootstrap not of your congruences;
this flirt with fate & her unskirted resolve:
this cleated slipper of glass; this broken
bottle with porting, majestic insole.

The Red Clay Ostraca Of Fayre Gabbro

i, too, was a mermaid in the muck, a maiden from the moon,
with banjo on my knee, like any capable wanderer.

in a cove of my own clawing, dug down into the toothsome dark
until shawled in the ambry of night—down there

with naught in the mythical larders i found a subterranean
whimsy—an excursion deep within,

a largesse of love; this philanthropy of self. and ever since,
i've been nothing but sun.

a perchance of blackness imbrued in those adorable depths.
my cavernous spirit a vast, yawning ambrosia.

i had to learn to see it, myself for myself; this unambiguous
yearning sprawling within my soul.

neither shameful nor slithering in the oil, but glistening. reach
into my scales for umbrageous glamour, for spells

reserved for campfire, the scalding cauldron, several cups
of tea, this petticoat from the ashes.

this slick and heavy indulgence, the mermaid with frolicking
grasp and dorsal fin and shimmering, igneous

skin. come with me into the trenches—the charmed pot, this untrou-
bled toil—and be with me, the fawn

with self-reflecting references, the high elegant heels,
the sheer backless gown, my hair

a cumulus chenille with its conquering logjam
corporeally tender towering above all.

Fayre Gabbro Travels Time To View The End Of Days

Strange, this fierce strong soaring
　　　　　—Gayl Jones, "Stranger"

Is this I? brown and vast and sweltering in cobalt.
in what century did my belly devour the moon?
i am my own earth, how monstrous my pulchritude,
with volcanos astriding my brow like a tiara . . .
this choreography of comets as crown, tachyons
erupting as sonnets from my forehead. . . . i am a small
dense sun! a white dwarf! and every solar system lain
at my feet like an endowment; this dowry at my death!

it will take millennia for the Milky Way to have trained
past my coffin, each star stopping to kiss my hand in casket;
oh, how the nebulae weep for me! and still yet I'm birthing
planets from the womb! each afterbirth its own atmosphere!
a nativity of meteorites and asteroids. . . . how many Gods
have grown complete and come undone in my shadows?
how many big bangs have baptized on my tongue, in my tears?
how did i grow to deserve such affection?
how incalculable the songs collected in the folds of my skin;
this orchestra of a trillion origins between my thighs . . .

quite the maestro i've become.
this nacreous black bauble born from a fog bank;
this black start diesel sheathed in a blanket of stars . . .
what a distance i've acquired, from Uhlanga to Eternity!
who knew the tip of my cutlass would be a fairy tale?
how did i ever come to pass: this pampered fable born
in a season of blood loss from a small drop of motor oil
hissing hotly in its clamshell.

how sublime, how supreme,
　　　　　　my joyous songs a sheen of stretch marks

across the breast meat of the universe.

i am fully seen. i am forever devoured.

and deep into the end of time, i crack open / only now.

Fayre Gabbro & The Fairy Tale's End
As Reported By The Poet Who Loved Her

the wolf that roamed these woods loved
Gabbro so much that villagers would
find her asleep in its mane, nestled
between tufts of sweet sultan, pillowed
atop garlands of globe thistle

she cast a fearsome shadow when straddled
upon her lycan steed, with every knight
& jackanapes at her heel. but last night, down
by the estuary, the wolf's head was found—
a stream of tears, wet & acrid, upon its cheek

her severed wrist cleaved & snarling from
its fangs, the dagger in her palm fanning sonnets
at the moon, the honey pouring from the wound
yet all-the-while fighting still with unseen forces;
and when the sun arose within the realm

every stalk of wheat burnt so green (to be
December) as ice on the trees set fire to itself
all at once as mynah wailed and choked out ashes:
every songbird in stark array / the air burnished
in softened ode, a detritus of verse—

"you should've seen it" the ravens sang,
a hallowness in their tears; *"you should've
seen it"* they cried their blackful burr
a perfect harrow trawling sorrows,
deep & taut, over lake & lea

and without a sovereign song the village
withered—never finch or crow to again
take wing. so the poet in distress declared
war upon his eyes, the brimstone

pouring from his emptied sockets:

he roamed every corner until (*in full*
descent, without the guide of muse or madness)
he burned the fields & took up sword,
he swallowed sea & became a king,
encysting world in rust & stone;

for gone was the seed for his conceit—
the Girl with the Tattoo of Frantz Fanon;
every ember on this stridden path weeping at
our loss—but could this be truly how
the story folds for our Wayfarer of All Rainforests,

Guardian of All Trenchant Beulahs? for our
Obinrin Lati Omi, the Boss Belle of Kirinyaga Woods?
surely, it's ill-come thinking this is how
her saga abates, because every fade to black
is not a loss in light but a thickening glaze—

the world, *by choice*, turning from its faience
to the dislimns of Love; but as any grizzled gawlo
knows after the vast eclipse a nascence always
follows: the peckish Day—*as composed by Night*—
ingests the carol then craves lament

& thus, in true, our tale begins; like a scent
of honey on the breath of a dying wolf.

THE
UNDERGROUND
RUBAIYAT

Tangerine Tubman

-KUIMBA: MDCCCLIII-

-1-

Ringing out, the twilight doesn't
stay soft for long; it sings out
to the credulous, rerouting the
curiosity of incredibly furious
men, where us Slivers of Africa
migrate a Telltale Path.

For such wayfarers, morning's
falsetto is an unraveling ray but
with our feet-to-the-wind we
are often the most fleet come
midnight—

Moon-crickets on the lamb
Bricks of gold on gifted wing.

Boughs ache & crack, bearing
this American weight, the
brunt equity of hate & power
distributing a colossal mass
foreign in appraisal—our heavy
gods as the masks we wear,
tutelary gods deemed ignoble by
paled, elite gradience; our black,
frothy hair swaying disconnected
from this specious heaven; our
bodies of light lost to flinching;
the black identity breached until
truth is contorted & clinging to
Dear Life for tender pride—&
it matters not which side of
the bough (above or below)—

equilibrium always comes
gleaning, a flabbergast leaching
until you end & the gristle of you
glistens in a bell jar.

For 300 years the elected branch
resists corrosion; balancing,
in sponsor, a commodity of
shadows: a one-sided-avarice vs.
the seeds of Kujichagulia.

. . .

Harriet, do you hear me?
I said I love you.

Her eyes proffer the crepuscular
"hush, fool" as she raises off
hip, reading topography of sky,
deciphering blueprint for our
relay-run—a wreath of thorns
& chicken wire surrounding
sunrise / halo for a long way to
go.

In this lean moment dark
eyes share discourse with
constellations, each iris a
perfectly tooled buckshot
drawing bead on morning
acclivity where every sight &
sound is strained or sieved
through experience & instinct;
her eyes cast from the hardest of
coals, (& sometimes, the softest);
I dare you to unconvince me.

Am I the fool for wanting? with
mouth waxing & actions waning?

I move by her side, my grateful hand a croaker sack against her graceful hip demanding their calloused fill of crocus & buttercup

—*I am the fool.*

200 feet off the plantation & every broken knave reinvents "nobility" (in past & present tense), proclaiming Harriet's invincibility to be his own creation, his brutally enslaved self-inflicted sense of grandeur—*there but for the Grace O' God go . . .*

I . . . Harriet?—*Harriet!*

Her iron hand forms an ancient vice across my mouth—a well-seasoned clamp of metal as biblical as a Passover; the plum of her palm a perfect muzzle & I am shushed; a silence that mimicks the fatal—*but what is it she stifles?*—my braying or the brazened nonsense of notions burrowed 'neath my brow until gushing?

From the underbrush she rises & assumes the bard's position, my supernal caryatid, squaring hips for soliloquy (or prophecy), where buttstock is both pulpit & witness—BlackMoses in full zenith, each tooth striking flint beneath a delta of dark eyes— She says / Harriet says to me:

Dare not think this small earthen'd patch is proper monument for our promises raw & new, not ever for a moment. large is Life & to love in it in incremental fragments is a fractured choice; this smallness is indeed a slave's acceptance—not the first link but the latch in our chains.

Previously hidden the sun bubbles up like blood from a stone, a soft sponge heavy with Nile cleansing what sores me; my soul swaddled by her reed of hands in which I'm finding too much comfort—why can't we, *as well,* lounge in fondnesses deprived of the circumstances for foreign ownership & its oversight?

. . .

Harriet's eyes, aquiver, see everything—all & at once: the sun & the shadowlands, the pain & the promises / Harriet is seven moves ahead of pitfall—the Master Strategist for Stolen Property; the underground's prima ballerina (our abolitional Marie Taglioni) dancing adagio through tobacco fields & high cotton
—*Crops de ballet.*

Harriet is America's Joan of Arc, the break of dawn flaring from her face—charging headlong, tho hidden, into the fray of our *Hundreds of Years War*.

Were she White, then Anglophiles with flute & lyre would mire her charms in nascent song, would laud her resolve with lilting refrain, famed as warrior-frail, this *odalisque-in-another-lifetime* embossed in gauze & silk, surrounded ankle to crown by suitor-kings with clots of handmaids & ostrich plumes in frame, fanning her pale sinewy ass: *Statuesque*—the bards would sing.

but she isn't White with the stalwart plight of *plum or peach* for breakfast; colonial tongues will only muster teeth-sucking / her name burning as phlegm on tongues—their mouths gaping like snaggle-toothed gates of Hell cattle-prodding law with language; her name a sour chaw they dare not swallow: *Stoic*—is the best they'll say, never heroic; their sense of romanticism stunted by courageous sable:

This God-given beast is strong of stock with good teeth & a thick neck. suited for thrashing seed from chaff, but can bleed a calf & knows her way around the kitchen. you can trust her with your progeny & whoever said she "isn't worth a sixpence" extols decisively in slander for this Mighty Negress is built for many, many burdens.

No.

They'll never label her—my dauntless love—*the lissome fawn,* cast in gouache & oil with garlands of gold embracing pate while morning's dew dampens the dark umbral clay of her soft-as-midnight brow; Harriet's florid areola winking at auditors beneath off-the-shoulder silk; no, she'll always be a single, archaic entry in every slaver's long-drawn-out ledger: *the wet nurse. the loyal servant. the very adequate cook.* the coruscant never seen in her eyes; the genteelness of her touch avoided except to herald the over-possessor's lust— abrasive words dismounting the African's defiant stance, but damn them that for Harriet is nonetheless—

Statuesque.

(Lord Jesus, when did I become this salacious penning rubaiyats for night-runners?)

Does the prospect of freedom,

this perchance at death make me so unafraid, wanting desires this unreserved? I'm ashamed not wanting this love to be adrenaline's rush or for Harriet's lithe touch to be ephemeral, tender & transient. Oh, Lord, who knew iron could be so delicate? but where Harriet's hands are soft, her dark nubilous gaze could kick-start a mule & in this moment her sights are drawn upon the gourd of my soul—within her eyes I am entirely devoured, spiraling fast into conjure & fabrication. Her palm to my chest: half corsage, half the throes-of-death—

Us people, us Us-people, need an entire Earth beneath them, not just the grass-stain swatch patched in convenience for our asses, not if we're to be the kind of love Our God intends. & it's not that I don't trust you, I'm just tired. I manage time; never have I tamed it; understand— not just be aware—my fear of alacrity (concerning Love), my kitchens are full of yeast & sweat & not yet enough cane, nor hardly any cinnamon & I will not bake my lover's bread in secret; the woman I am must always be on guard & strong enough to keep bloodshed from the bedroom. Lord knows, this way of life offers no easy staples for new love, not when it barely feeds

itself. & as long as we are enslaved then we are at war—we are free spirits, not ghosts / behoven & we, too, deserve the good things. but for the resolute of us to chase "something more" then a small sum must embrace the phantasms; be as bridges between the chasms. & if you think that makes me excessively hardened as a Black Woman then you mistake being Unchained as being Free & you'll die some nigger- fool regardless to the richness of soil beneath your feet.

A wrought spell her deepest whisper.

. . .

The salted black scar is forced into the shape of the South's asphyxiating smile & i'm of little help offering no intimate sovereignty for our hopes & fears; this cooing demeanor as the only means of defense; all I can do is—run—now, what infernal mean designs such a man?—the hare placed in snares made for the fox then told to never howl, told to never curl its lip & yet we are the hare—so this cleft in our smile is natural.

But with shoes torn & overrun I remove a pebble; hands that crave the carving of soapstone into memory are too busy mending sackcloth into the impromptu rites of an incomplete culture.

What incessantly boils in this nebulous brine, from every corner of these cold colonies, is the bone marrow of our seasoned elders; in its pickled prime the fermented black skin is their perfect prize, its mineral ores battled for, bottled & bartered over, barreled then sold to the highest bidder—fodder for the South's spoiled, specious gods; their preciously mottled Gods: their blotters throbbing with our flesh, robbing us / rubbing us away . . . but what use now—this rehashing of over-known histories beneath heaven's open court? after all of this forced, vapid descent has not the proper din been justifiably heard? we have sang & shouted for heavenly salvations.

Harriet would never have it, but to The Gods of Inherited Fear I say—*Fuck you*—eye glinting against eye.

. . .

But what makes Lady Harriet an underived hero? at emergent heartbeat's primal request / without hint of hesitation, she legislates every goal: without err she calculates the dangerous choice to full conclusion; even her walk propagates freedom— you can not unsee it: our double-agent, sainted prototype suffragist. our perennial secret weapon; Black Knight in Midnight's Armor. Our defense attorney against their cooing clucks; armed. straightforward. steady & supple.

. . .

What fool would not follow into battle such an unassuming beauty? I've saturated myself, like September's aurelian turn, with her every keloid—the verdant seized by the auric; sank kisses blistering into skin; each welt on her backside slobbered in love; my spirit inflated by her pyretic touch; my heart, unsated like the over-demanding entity it becomes in her presence. Mount Kenya is not this majestic & in that truth, Queen Mother Moses is unmatched.

Truth be told: Harriet Tubman is my Lord & Savior. for who abandons Joy when it topples them? Isn't this how Genocide is overcome / how Apocalypse is overturned? this braiding of ascension into world-ending dystopia.

. . .

We flatten into the heath—
"Hush. Or I'll kill you; disaster brays & hounds are near."

(I want to reply "yes, woman, **I know!**"—lashing out in the vacuous tone gifted us by overseers rummaging through my head, but Harriet's stare remains an exorcism; only when she blinks is it safe of me to breathe & to the roots of the underbrush my shadow binds me; but oh, how flustered I am. & frail—so much to overcome in true deliverance, our run—*within*—the run.)

Tonight we camp in quiet & dine on stress; companions in shared anxiety.

-2-

The aura of desire is as dust for The shackled & the sly; but still, instead of being weary, I worry for her.

. . .

There is no time to waste, measuring & debating the merits of *rest* vs. *waiting*; a penumbral heaven might pinch us below from squinting eyes, but not our stench from hounds. It's a compromise of time, dallying in tenderness; we are as gazelles, heads bowed in drink near bodies of water with crocodiles hidden in the rim—the shackle-toothed wyverns / slavers on patrol with the piety of piranhas; their devout faith pompous in circumstance for they alone take luxury appeasing hunger with patience but us having wet, doe-eyes wide with grace will not forestall them dining on our radiance.

. . .

no matter what their manuals say, you never grow accustomed to holocaust. The cat-o'-nine-tails is not the savior they say it is wedding us to complacent conversion; force any man to graze on slavery & he will always hate the nature of gravity.

What a broken pathos these White people have to bar us from our own exemplifying beauty.

But not even the orchestrated fear of being dehumanized by white hands or the assurances of being fatally hobbled by Harriet are negative enough portents to prevent my mind from rambling: last night, Harriet was my obeah; a quintessence / a much-needed nectar & my Fruit of Life; Harriet The Redolent, Harriet The Dulcet, but what fugitive brakes, positing his Grand Desire in romantic prose?—*a dead one!*

& what solid wealth is a slave's token tongue promising a lifetime of liberty to a woman obsessed, defying the gallows as she harvests freedom-for-all? what superpowers can a simple fool possess enough of to pull her away from the plight of her people weighted in carnage by the Gatekeepers of Civility?

What, if not this now of now / this hidden glade instead a glamour & my hazy glance upon her dew a remedial faint repose or romance blooming in fastidious shadow, a bright untethered nowness anew—a bravery without cowl or brevity . . . to kiss without scorn or scurge, the sudden flare of come hither a soft fury without fetter . . . tho not a what or even when-if / a why not?—such a forge addresses the debt. & Sweet Jehovah, why shouldn't it?

I raggedly sigh, sagging into this forced-upon subculture christened by The Unkept as "The Natural State of the Negro in Counterfeit Humanity."

. . .

We move on & merge ahead with others on the darkest side of John Brown's barn. Harriet assures us

freedom will be followed to the very letter, leaving no easy trail for the patewallers in pursuit:

Die free. Or die a fatality.

Doubt her? there is always a firearm at her fingertips for she is as cruel as need demands, so intentively we adhere (*especially as the sonnets erected in gun smoke above the ashes of a Negro campsite are seldom merciful or kind*).

-3-

Run—now!—long, hard, & fast: this simple trope / this motion towards salvation is all there is of Africa on either side of the Mason-Dixon. we struggle fair & *if lucky* we die clean; stopping to care for a wound to your head or to cry for the soul will cost you the skin on your back; your split-open head a garden apple on the tree of *you should've rested once you was free, nigger!*

But Harriet's smile is my psalm; I love you, Harriet. Harriet—
    I know you hear me.

The gaze she returns ignites all gunpowder, cauterizing my emotional wound; a soldering to my larynx—they say it's not the thirst that kills you during drought, but (when the heavens break & the waters come) your drinking too much, too soon that ruins you & this threat of rain, this consistent running, is a cold precipitation—Saint Harriet is a hurricane walking, a tornado on your side until you take her thunderstorm for granted.

. . .

At the river's edge, we wade the shallows; we board barely-a-boat & squat low concealed within the shadows of freight.

Harriet, her charge done, stays on the bank changing charades, assuming a docile, surrendered shape. the Whites call her *colored* but we all know her as Queen Chameleon.

Done heard about the many who go down drowning, running on water like a Mississippi Miracle, those *momentary messiahs* go down slow, *drapetomaniacs* to the core until death—that, before asphyxiating on tears with hands & feet sheared as preventive cure by the anti-emancipation mendicants "healing" us our habitual relapses, spiritually drowning in the evening sky; obituary will still say you died a slave—less obituary, more a loss-of-property—buckra's insurance claim extending from your toe—in the Bible, Moses parted the waters, never does it say he swam a sea for freedom, choking, in the end, on desperation in midstream, in mid-stroke.

It hasn't yet come down to that for Harriet, this freedom-chase hasn't failed her yet. in fact, the fabled *Titanic* will to disaster itself surrender just 329 days before Harriet gently succumbs.

Harriet—*The Sovereign Tip Of Freedom's Iceburg.*

. . .

Seconds are roughly shared on the riverbank for softness, my sense of passion is again optimal & for a moment our absolutisms dissolve / lips tremble in the want to say & do more / there is treble; & just like the dawn my faith in her too sings falsetto . . .

I am hummingbird for Harriet.

. . .

*One day, God made a plan & the next we—WE!—bade Him to another—& **He obeyed**. We, Black, embody myth & Movement, so Lover, never mourn. My mother named me* Araminta, Minta, *her spoils from "The Confederacy," an old-timey play from long ago.*

So recall fondly, your Minta &
remember her as she'll remember
you, for the time'll come when two is
less than one, our twaining undone.
You see, Time & Freedom are but
rejoinders of God's Good Love &
All-The-Else-That-We-Desire—our
bodies rising slowly for the Sun &
bating quickly with the Night.

-4-

& there at the end of dawn,
with the dew of freedom fresh
upon my lips & desires veiled
across the Iroquois lawn with
African hands stern & apt upon
the rudder, My Fae Dark Steed
turned again the Vesperous Fawn
& I to ancient ore with peacock's
quill within my grip: *Harriet &*
I parted ways—my trembling
limbs freer than this fluttering
song, an illegal lyricism not yet
allowed *(if ever)* to vibrantly ode
in America's vast, wide open; a
kinetic song I hope not returned
to in doom as some chewed-over
rejoinder but as discernible idyll
nesting within the cries of our
babies—for *what other* purpose
emancipation?

. . .

We misappraise our very nature
to Love, disregarding its lineage
to Liberty.

The End

Appearances & Acknowledgments

"Spaceship For Sale" and "Fayre Gabbro Travels Time To View The End of Days" appear in *The Future of Black: Afrofuturism, Black Comics, and Superhero Poetry,* Blair, 2021

"To Stand Down (And To Stand By)" appears in *Black Writing on Nature,* Pangyrus, 2021

"Fayre Gabbro & The Reclamation of Time" appears in *Protean Magazine,* January, 2022

"Fayre Gabbro In The Orchard" appears in *What Things Cost: an anthology for the people,* University Press of Kentucky, 2023

"Fayre Gabbro In The Land Of Isle Iffy," "Fayre Gabbro & The Trickster God Dossier," "Fayre Gabbro & The Fairy Tale's End," and "Fayre Gabbro & The Duppy Of Dreams Epistolary" are forthcoming online at Ice Floe Press, 2023

"Abstrack Africana" and "John Henry Says I Am Not My Hammer" appear in *Hayden's Ferry Review,* January, 2023

"The Canticle Of Fayre Gabbro" and "Fayre Gabbro, The Woman In The Sun" are forthcoming, print and/or online, with Pangyrus, 2023

Earlier versions of "A Blues For Eunice Waymon," "When All Is Ready, I Throw This Switch" (as "Gawlology 101"), "The Death Of Olympia," "The Night Of The Purple Moon," and "Bleeding The Calf" all appear in the chapbook *Caul & Response,* Argus House Press, 2015

An earlier version of "Tangerine Tubman" appears in the self-titled chapbook, *Left-Handed,* Juju Press, 2016

"Myth • Theory • Us / Dear Crys:" appears as "Myth-Theory-Us" in the collection *To Emit Teal,* Broadstone Books, 2020.

THE GLOAMING ATLANTIC BLACKOUT

—1, 2, 3.

Myth • Theory • Us / Dear Crys:

1.

i toss the lion's paws upon the kitchen table,
its tail in a soup pot with beans and rice;
its head i wear, my heroic eyes peering through
its maw, a tiara of teeth / its tongue slung
       like a sideburn askew:

       Champion of the Gods,
    i was born with a slivered moon in my mouth.

Demon Tamer. Storm Slayer. Soothsayer. Fannie Lou
Hamer tattooed on my ass's jawbone. and when i roar
a swarm of lightning bugs foam from my mouth
soaring into the sky until all is overcast and dark
      portentous by my own doing.

this intaglio of tea leaves as folklore in your tea cup:

      "a trouble is a-brew"

2.

i come, in love, to you; my heart
folded over into this tannery of pillow talk.
my lungs a sheath for all your loose skin.
my entire mouth a mortar for your spells;
sugar, come & grind all of your spices here.

the skull bone of a foreign love god
is my cereal bowl but there's no sweetness

to the grains within, so let me steep you
in this morning's milk until your comb swells and
the honey comes. for i know, in you, there is honey

3.

a centuries-ago prophecy sent me
to your door and i smell the apiary you sleep in
on your gown. even in your shadow
there is sorghum. meniscus, tendons, and gristle;
not one empty calorie . . .

i heel at your knee; feasting.

4.

the 365 Labors of Kereenyaga Heru

each day i contend with throngs to keep you
safe. happy. and draped in desire.
i whittle mountains down into a bust of you,
placing each atop a pedestal, or a pyramid,
or a milk crate . . . your umbrageous charm, to me,
an ivory tower; this silhouette of us
is a constellational song.

the lion's growl—*my lamentation*—creeping;
with the husk of me at your heels, weeping.
i came to this Haven to reap & pillage

i end each day in your lap,
playing with your yarns.

The Sunken Treasure Of Fayre Gabbro

adrift at ocean's bottom—a corpse of sun and still
the blossoming moon within bosom tho your entire
beauty encrusted lays in silt & salt the seismic

a faultline of apprizements oh how the Gods
in continuance cry at such unexalted sacrifices
the Pangaea of your song the Gondwana of your hips

as fuselages for all things civilized might as well
however be a plastic isle in the debris of history a
jettison on any appetite for romance—and yet your

corneas gilded by sun still pierce Heaven eyes opened
& unrestricted to the liaisons of freshwatered Love
—the gloaming Atlantic blackout of your Love

Amen / Ashé / Hey Now
after Haki & Safisha's Love / For CW

we have earthquakes to perform
rituals for sunrise to maintain
from starcore Auset
to yamroot underground

   —black voice be vein to universe

our broken verbs african & vestal
demanding sacrifice these dark
tongues of ours *sweet woman*
wreaking havoc until neon

About the Author

 **upfromsumdirt**, Ron Davis, is an autodidactic poet and award-winning visual artist based in Lexington, Kentucky. He is the author of two previous poetry collections, *Deifying a Total Darkness* and *To Emit Teal*, and is currently storyboarding a graphic novel based on his poetry. He has also published works in anthologies and periodicals including *The Future of Black: Afrofuturism, Black Comics, and Superhero Poetry*; *Anthology of Appalachian Writers*; *Hayden's Ferry Review*; and more. He received the Kentucky Al Smith Award in Art in 2010 and the Southeastern Libraries Association Award for Excellence in Original Artwork in 2022. His artwork is also featured in the NAACP Image Award–winning poetry collection *Perfect Black* by Crystal Wilkinson and *A Is for Affrilachia* by Frank X Walker. He was inducted as a member into the Affrilachian Poets in 2022.